Lark's gaze narrowed. "If I agree to a date, will you kiss me already?"

"If you say yes—" he teased a touch along her plump lower lip "—I'll kiss you until you ask me to stop."

She gave a small nod, sealing the deal.

"You made me a very happy man tonight." Gibson still wrestled with the urge to run his hands all over her, but at least he had the green light for taking that sweet, sweet mouth of hers.

He closed the last of the distance between them, her curves brushing against him.

"So start making me a very happy woman." Her clear-eyed challenge was meant to goad him into taking her hard and fast.

She had to know how much he wanted that.

But he wouldn't mess up this chance with her by rushing or taking more than what they'd agreed on.

"Soon enough. I promise..."

* * *

A Colorado Claim by Joanne Rock
is part of the Return to Catamount series.

Dear Reader,

Welcome back to Catamount, Colorado, a place I've loved calling home this year. The Barclay sisters have found places in my heart, especially Lark, the practical one who hides a romantic streak beneath her no-nonsense approach to life. I had fun figuring out what kind of hero would turn her head while she charges through life getting things done.

Enter Gibson Vaughn, who hasn't gotten over his ex-wife, even if he's still stinging from the fact that she walked away. He thinks he's moved on until he runs into her outside of a Colorado courthouse, a meeting that stirs too many unhappy memories of their divorce.

But second chances happen in real life, even for couples who seem like the unlikeliest of matches. Opposites often attract because their opposing traits balance one another out. Or maybe they just create an irresistible spark! For Lark and Gibson, it might be a little of both. I hope you'll cheer them on as they fight their way back to one another.

Happy reading!

Joanne Rock

JOANNE ROCK

A COLORADO CLAIM

HARLEQUIN
DESIRE

ISBN-13: 978-1-335-58128-0

A Colorado Claim

Recycling programs for this product may not exist in your area.

Harlequin Enterprises ULC
22 Adelaide St. West, 40th Floor
Toronto, Ontario M5H 4E3, Canada
www.Harlequin.com

Printed in U.S.A.

Joanne Rock credits her decision to write romance after a book she picked up during a flight delay engrossed her so thoroughly that she didn't mind at all when her flight was delayed two more times. Giving her readers the chance to escape into another world has motivated her to write over eighty books for a variety of Harlequin series.

Books by Joanne Rock

Harlequin Desire

Dynasties: Mesa Falls

The Rebel
The Rival
Rule Breaker
Heartbreaker
The Rancher
The Heir

Return to Catamount

Rocky Mountain Rivals
One Colorado Night
A Colorado Claim

Visit her Author Profile page at Harlequin.com, or joannerock.com, for more titles.

You can also find Joanne Rock on Facebook, along with other Harlequin Desire authors, at Facebook.com/harlequindesireauthors!

For my one and only,
very best sister, Linda Watson.

One

Normally, Los Angeles-based child psychologist Lark Barclay wouldn't have wasted a Thursday afternoon daydreaming about her next adult beverage.

Today wasn't any ordinary Thursday.

And not just because she'd flown halfway across the country to be seated in a Routt County, Colorado, courtroom between the sisters she'd barely spoken to in the past decade. No, this afternoon was also different because she'd rescheduled all of her client appointments for a two-week stretch to be present at this all-important probate hearing. She hated rescheduling, taking great care to accommodate vulnerable patients who relied on her help. Yet she'd shuffled her schedule anyhow to show solidarity with her estranged siblings and to finally—*finally*—achieve a long overdue victory in an ongoing battle with her self-centered prick of a father.

Except her father hadn't shown up to today's hearing. Even though *he'd* been the one to contest his mother's will to prevent his daughters from inheriting Crooked Elm Ranch. The judge had informed Lark, Jessamyn and Fleur Barclay that their dad's attorney had requested a continuance because they needed more time to build their case, and the judge had granted it.

Cue the need for day drinking.

"The bastard," Jessamyn muttered under her breath after the judge refused to delay the trial for the requested three weeks but did grant a one-week delay. Younger than Lark by four years, Jessamyn was the middle child who'd never acted like one. The peace-keeping role in the Barclay clan belonged to their baby sister, Fleur, while Jessamyn was more apt to kick ass and take names. "He couldn't have given us a heads-up that he was trying to delay the hearing?"

The judge moved on to the next case on her docket, freeing the Barclay sisters to leave the courtroom.

Lark, leading the way between the benches toward the exit, bit her tongue to prevent herself from responding to her sister's gripe. Jessamyn had been their father's protégé in his real estate development business, only recently coming around to recognizing what an underhanded tool Mateo Barclay could be. It galled Lark a little that Jessamyn had netted huge financial gains by closing her eyes to the truth of their father's character for most of their lives.

But Lark had promised Fleur that she would give Jessamyn a chance to prove she'd changed, a promise Lark took all the more seriously since Jessamyn had learned she was pregnant. How could she hassle an expectant mom? So Lark held in the damning words she would have preferred to speak, all the while hoping she'd spot a bar across the street once they left this godforsaken courthouse. Preferably one with a two-for-one happy hour special.

"It's fine that he postponed," Lark told Jessamyn, willing the words to be true. "The extra week gives us more time to prepare, too."

Even as the added days away from her practice could do harm to her patients. She made a mental note to increase her hours allotted for telehealth visits this week to cover the gap. At least the judge had listened to their attorney's objection that the sisters—namely Lark—could not remain in Catamount indefinitely. She had a life in Los Angeles to get back to once she settled her family affairs.

Then, shoving open the door to exit probate court, she entered the long, echoing corridor connecting that room to many more in the historic Routt County building. Marble floors stretched in either direction, while the ornate molding around every door gleamed. A few people milled outside other courts in session, including the men who waited for her sisters: Drake Alexander, a Catamount, Colorado, native and former bull rider who'd fallen hard for Lark's sister Fleur, and Ryder Wakefield, a search and rescue volunteer who had recently renewed a relationship with Jessamyn.

Well, more than *renewed*, since Ryder was the father of the child Jessamyn carried.

Since they were being called as witnesses, they hadn't come into the court. But clearly both Drake and Ryder were good, upstanding men. Wealthy, too. Exceedingly so. Too bad it was still tough for Lark to witness the electric emotions of new lovers as the pairs greeted one another. Her own failure in that department stung. Glancing away from the sappy reunions, Lark turned her gaze farther down the high-ceilinged corridor to where a mother entertained a toddler with a storybook. Next to her, a weather-beaten older man slumped on a wooden bench, absorbed in a racing form.

And, closer to Lark, a young couple dressed in matching suits with contrasting boutonnieres stared into one another's eyes, clearly on the verge of speaking marriage vows.

The sight of the pair, practically glowing with dreams for their future, provided one final gut-punch on a day already filled with cheap shots. Because Lark had been part of a couple like that once, standing beside a man she'd loved, ready to take on the world armed with nothing but foolish hope and romantic fantasies.

The memory of her short and ill-fated marriage to hockey star Gibson Vaughn sent a bitter pain through her breast even though they'd been divorced for just over two years. Twenty-six months and two days, if she was counting. Which, okay, maybe she was. But only because she didn't take it for granted that she'd been liberated from the sports media limelight ever since their split.

Free of stupid headlines about hockey's most eligible bachelor marrying a no-nonsense therapist. Free of insinuations that her superstar ex had tied himself to a hockey club with no playoff hopes to appease a bride who refused to relocate her therapy practice. Free of toxic social media comments about Gibson's dating life before he'd married her.

None of which would have bothered her if Gibson had spent even a quarter of the year with her. But the prolonged absences from home necessitated by his desire to prove himself the face of his team chipped away the foundations of their relationship. He hadn't been there when she'd needed him most.

"Lark?" Fleur's gentle voice broke through Lark's unhappy trip down memory lane. Her copper-haired sister turned gray eyes on her, still as lovely as when she'd won rodeo queen titles all over the West. "Did you want to go for a late lunch with us?"

Dragging her gaze from the husbands-to-be down the hall, Lark swallowed the regrets about her own marriage, determined to follow through on her solo plans for the afternoon. She hadn't hit a bar alone in years and this day had her feeling all kinds of edgy. Right now, she considered a tequila shot and beer chaser to be critical self-care.

"No, thank you." Lark flipped her heavy braid of dark hair behind one shoulder as she took in the sight of her sisters in love. Drake and Fleur had their arms around one another's waists, while Jessamyn's fingers laced securely through Ryder's. "I need to—" she hesitated, unwilling to share the sad truth that she couldn't abide being around the overload of love and hormones that oozed from every one of the four people in front of her "—check in with a client. I'll see you at Crooked Elm tonight."

Making a show of digging in her bag for her phone, Lark gave a half-hearted wave to her sisters as they departed with their respective men.

Once they were gone, Lark used her search browser to find the closest dive bar and found a likely candidate within walking distance. If she couldn't enjoy a courtroom victory over her lying cheat of a father today, she would use her rare time out of the office to indulge in something else that would bring her satisfaction.

Or maybe she needed to drink away the memories that being in a courtroom inevitably reawakened.

Like the day she'd stood in front of a judge and uttered the words, "irreconcilable differences." The death knell of her marriage to Gibson, and all the hopes and dreams that had gone with it.

Fueled with purpose, she jammed the device in her utilitarian cross-body bag. Was her purse a designer original? Not on a therapist's salary. Not with all her student loans. Was it even remotely feminine or delicate? Not for a woman who prized functionality above appearances.

Marching toward the exit with extra stomp in her step, she gave a polite nod to the security guards who worked the metal detector. Then, pushing her way out into the warm summer sunshine, she blinked at the small throng of people standing at the base of the courthouse steps.

Why did they look vaguely familiar?

She was certain she didn't recognize any of them in particular. But as a group, they stirred something in her memory.

The thought troubled her while she descended the stone steps. A moment later, vaguely registering the sound of the courtroom doors opening and closing behind her, she saw the small crowd move as one.

Coming toward her.

Lifting cameras she hadn't noticed before.

A moment's confusion faded as it occurred to her why the group looked familiar. Flashbacks to her former life scrolled through her brain as she recognized the scavenger behavior of reporters in "entertainment media."

And if they were here, it could only be to hound someone famous. Someone who, she slowly realized, must be behind her.

A sickening foreboding clamped her stomach in a fist. Catamount, Colorado only had so many celebrity residents.

Even as Lark thought it, she heard the first shout rise from the crowd of so-called journalists.

"Gibson! Over here, Gibson!" a woman's voice called from the left. "Can you tell us what you're doing at a courthouse?"

Gibson.

Lark froze in place on the stairs. Unable to take another step forward. Or backward.

Sort of like she'd been in the two years since her divorce.

Another reporter crowded closer, almost knocking Lark over as he lifted a boom mic above her head to a point behind her. "Gibson, is it true you're going to reconcile with your ex-wife?" the man shouted.

Cameras whirred, flashes popping in a strobe light effect that catapulted her back to some of the most infuriating moments of her life. Being caught on film at the grocery store at midnight when she'd needed supplies to help a scared mother and her daughter to escape a dangerous partner. Being hounded about Gibson's activities on a team road trip while Lark was in Los Angeles at a homeless shelter to advocate for one of her young patients.

But she couldn't think about that now when—impossibly—her ex-husband obviously stood behind her. She should pull a legger, dart away before anyone with a camera realized that the same "ex-wife" they were asking about stood just a few feet away.

For once, she was grateful her unmemorable looks had failed to draw attention since no one seemed to have made the connection. Yet.

Her sense of self-preservation kicking in, Lark ducked her head and shifted left, sidestepping the throng while all eyes were trained somewhere else. Their raised voices drowned out every other sound, even the thudding of her heart and—thankfully—the sound of her ex's voice if he bothered to respond to the questions. Even his voice was sexy, damn him. She pounded down the stairs, skirting the group, never looking back as she headed for the parking area. Screw the bar. She needed her car to escape.

Except, *crap*.

She'd left her rented vehicle on the other side of the building, only walking out the front entrance because her map app had pointed her this way toward the dive bar. Halting beside an extended cab pickup truck, she resisted the urge to look over her shoulder to possibly catch a glimpse of Gibson.

Think, think, think.

Squeezing her temples between her thumb and forefinger, she tried to settle her racing pulse. Told herself the reporters wouldn't have seen her. That, more importantly, Gibson Vaughn hadn't seen her. Had he?

A sudden clamor rose near the courthouse again. Lark glanced around to see the mob shifting in the opposite direction from her, like a swarm in pursuit of a new hive. Gibson must have moved away.

Lucky for her, he'd taken the mob with him.

Steadying herself with one hand on the gray fender of the big pickup truck, she wondered if she'd really escaped the media mayhem. Since when was she that fortunate?

Better yet, she'd dodged seeing her ex.

Shoulders slumping with relief, she debated returning to her car now. Would the path be paparazzi-free?

Adjusting the strap of her cross-body bag, she stepped out of the shadows of the pickup just as a low-slung sports car spun into view. Lark didn't need to see through the heavily tinted windows to know who would be behind the wheel of a Porsche 911 in a shade she happened to know was called Adriatic Blue.

Her gut sank to her feet as the driver's side window lowered.

Gibson Vaughn, in all his sexy glory, appeared in the driver's seat. From his dark, shoulder length hair that begged a woman's fingers to come through it to the kissable dent centered in his chin, the man had been the face of US hockey for nearly a decade for a reason. He not only played the game with a vengeance, but he was undeniably handsome. The scar through one eyebrow and the slight crook in his nose didn't begin to detract from those chiseled good looks.

"We've got about twenty seconds before they catch up." Gibson nodded toward the mob of reporters at the courthouse steps, all still looking in the wrong direction. "Hop in if you want to stay a step ahead of them."

She wished that her heartbeat skipped because she was panicked about being caught in the limelight again. But she knew perfectly well the erratic pulse and humming in her veins was all owing to the man who'd once vowed to love her forever. The man whose kisses had turned her inside out.

No way could she risk being close to him again.

"What will it be, Lark?" His voice broke through her scattered memories, terse and deep, while the engine of his high performance car purred with the promise of a fast getaway. "They're coming."

Why, in that moment, she chose to peer backward like Orpheus turning to see Eurydice, Lark couldn't have said. But the sight of the small group running with their microphones and recording equipment finally got her in motion. Especially when someone shouted, "Lark! Lark Barclay, have you reconciled with Gibson?"

She'd been recognized.

Another, deeper voice called, "Will you convince him to return to hockey?"

Her throat dried up. And this time, her speeding pulse had everything to do with panic.

Better to risk the emotional fallout of spending time with Gibson than to be surrounded by her old enemy the sports press.

Launching forward, she rounded the vehicle and flung open the passenger door before heaving herself inside the air-conditioned interior.

A second later, Gibson punched the gas, hurtling them out of the parking lot and away from the cameras. Her relief lasted for about a nanosecond before Gibson's silky baritone filled the coupe.

"It's good to see you again, Lark."

Judging by how fast her head whipped around, her forest-green eyes narrowing at him, Gibson would have thought he'd insulted Lark.

But then, hadn't that always been the way between them? He'd continually been a step behind his razor-sharp ex-wife, too consumed with his career to give her the time she deserved, and too slow to understand her moods and needs.

Except, of course, for one sort of need. They'd been remarkably in tune sexually no matter how much the rest of their relationship fell apart. And how was it he'd wound up thinking about *that* ten seconds after seeing her for the first time in two years?

She looked incredible, of course. Her minimalist wardrobe—a taupe-colored skirt and chestnut brown boots with a white button down today—always let the woman shine and not the clothes. Her one sexy accessory was her long, dark hair woven into a thick braid.

"Did I say something wrong?" he asked, pinning his eyes to the road and keeping them there. He headed west, ready to put distance between them and the media hounds sniffing out a story about his retirement.

In his peripheral vision, he could see Lark leaning into the leather seat, hear her heavy plait falling from her shoulder to rest beside her with a soft *thunk*. He had fond memories of the silky mane rarely seen loose. He'd found it sexy as hell to be the man who saw her undone at the end of a day.

"Just surprised you'd be glad to see me after the way we parted." Her voice always had a note of authority in it, like she'd never second-guessed herself in her life. He'd always assumed that it must be reassuring for her patients, who had to trust in her judgment. "You told me it would be best not to contact each other anymore."

Ah, damn. Just hearing his emotional words flung at him dragged him to the past and that painful day when she'd ended their marriage. His fingers flexed against the steering wheel as he turned onto the road that would lead to Catamount.

"I didn't mean we shouldn't ever speak again," he clarified, checking his rearview mirror to make sure they weren't followed. "At the time, I'd hoped taking a breather from one another would make it easier for us both to move on."

In the silence that followed, he mentally laid odds on her response. Something sharp without being downright cutting. He could envision her perfectly, recalling the way she preferred the thoughtful consideration of her words over blurting out anything to fill a conversational void. His gaze might be on the county route winding alongside the Yampa River, but his mind's eye saw only Lark, her lips pursed in thought.

Which led him to think about her mouth and how she never wore lip color. He'd loved that about her, the way she never hid behind makeup, never felt the need to camouflage herself. With Lark, you got exactly what you saw, and when it came to her lush mouth, that was an excellent thing. Her lips required no help to be seductive.

And the lack of cosmetics made it simpler to taste *her*.

"Did it?" she asked softly, her thoughtful tone surprising him as much as the question itself. "Did the absence of contact make moving on easier for you?"

The confidential note in her voice catapulted him back to late night pillow talk. Long distance calls from the road when he'd been in some nameless hotel with the team, and she would pick up the phone even if she were half-asleep to ask him about his day. Why hadn't he asked about hers more often? Why hadn't he thought to put her first in his life?

"Tough to say since it was still...difficult," he admitted, downshifting as he slowed for a stop sign. "But I thought maintaining a friendship would only make it harder to get over you."

He'd been vocal about wanting to stay together. To work through her problems with his career. But there had been more to it than that, and he'd never been able to pin down what had been the final straw for her. She'd always kept some part of herself tightly closed. She'd given him her body, but he'd never been sure what was going on in her mind. One day, he'd returned to their Los Angeles home from an eleven-day road trip through Canada and she'd had her bags packed.

That had been the second worst day of his life, topped only by the last time they'd been in a courtroom together to dissolve their brief marriage. He couldn't bear a repeat of that pain, her rejection rattling him to the core. He hated failing at anything. From when he was young and his father abandoned the family, his job was to fix things for the people he cared about. His family and teammates. But Lark didn't need any fixing. And it had left him unsettled—not always in a good way.

"Right." She bit out the word, a chill creeping into her voice as she shifted in her seat. "You didn't want us to be friends. So why bother offering me a ride when the wolves are at our heels, all thanks to your decision to retire in Catamount? It wasn't difficult enough when we both lived in LA? Now we need to be neighbors here?"

Gibson ground his teeth together as he accelerated.

"I like Catamount. And just because I couldn't handle a friendship two years ago doesn't mean I would allow those reporters to hassle you. I know how much you value your privacy." All of which was true.

Yet, as he glanced her way again, his gaze snagged on the vee of her blouse and the shadowed patch of skin that hinted at her cleavage without being revealing. And he acknowledged that part of the reason he'd offered her a ride today was because he'd been floored to see her again.

He'd been in the Routt County Courthouse to establish conservatorship of his mother, who suffered from dementia. And he'd recognized Lark immediately, even from twenty-five yards behind her. Her all-business walk. Her feminine shape that her conservative outfits could never fully hide. And that perfectly straight hair, plaited with precision and clamped with a soft scrap of white cotton instead of a hair tie.

He'd tied those thin strips of cloth himself many times in the past, and he happened to know that it protected her from tresses from split ends. Watching the braid sway ever so slightly while she walked had been his downfall today, distracting him from the sports media who'd been lying in wait for him. How the hell had they learned he'd be in court today? He needed to keep out of the news cycle, damn it.

"In that case, thank you for the lift." She reached for the air vent and tilted it to blow higher on her face. "I want no part of the spotlight."

He didn't blame her. The media hadn't been kind to her. In an effort to shift the conversation away from unhappy memories, he asked, "Should I take you to Crooked Elm? Or do you need to return to the courthouse later? If we wait half an hour, the press will clear out."

"My car is back there, but I'd rather not chance returning for it." Folding her arms, she crossed her legs at the same time, her body language broadcasting how much she'd rather be almost anywhere besides in this car with him. "If you don't mind dropping me off at Crooked Elm, I'll ride in with my sisters tomorrow."

"Not a problem. I'm headed home anyway." The ranch he'd bought for his retirement from hockey shared a property line with the Barclay land, in fact, so taking her home couldn't be easier. He remembered from their talks before they split that she wasn't happy he'd decided to keep the home they'd once planned to live in together.

When she spoke again, her words were clipped, cool. "I appreciate it, Gibson. But this should be the last we see of each other while I'm in town. As you pointed out two years ago, there's no need to maintain a friendship."

Way to draw the battle lines, Lark.

He shouldn't be surprised, and yet the pinch of disappointment caught him off guard. He *had* moved on since their divorce, hadn't he? He'd dated, but nothing serious, and no one around here.

"If that's your preference, I'll certainly honor it," he said carefully, driving around a tractor with tires that spilled over into the opposite lane. "But let me know if you need any help managing the media."

She pivoted in her seat, her arms wrapping tighter around her midsection. "What do you mean?"

"You heard them back there. They recognized you. I'm sure someone snapped a photo of us together before you got into the car." He wasn't sure why she'd looked at the reporters when he'd offered her the ride, but then, her life hadn't involved ducking the media for the past two years so maybe she'd forgotten the drill.

Head bent. Avoid. Avoid. Avoid.

Her small moan of dismay was so unlike the self-possessed woman he recalled from their marriage, that he did a double take. Had that sound emanated from Lark Barclay?

And how wrong was it for him to feel a sharp bolt of need to inspire that sound again—for purely carnal reasons?

"I forgot about that," she admitted, seeming to recover herself. Or at least, she shifted to look out the window again, away from him. "But I'm sure I'll be fine."

With an effort, he swallowed the urge to pull the car over and face her head-on. He wanted to look into those forest-green eyes. Try to read what was going on in her thoughts. Or maybe finally understand what had happened to send her running from their marriage.

"I heard about your father contesting your grandmother's will." He'd liked Antonia Barclay tremendously. She was strong, feisty and endlessly competent, managing a large property on her own long after her family had left the area. During the occasional visits he made to Catamount to set up his home here, she had encouraged him to try his hand at ranching even after things went to hell between him and Lark. "I assume you'll be at the courthouse again soon. And there's a good chance the sports media will figure that out too, so they could be waiting to ambush you next time. If there's anything I can do—"

"Definitely not." She reached into the small brown bag she carried at her hip and withdrew her cellphone, an obvious social cue that she was done with the conversation. "Whatever happens, I'll handle it. Alone."

Same as ever.

Gibson increased his speed and refocused on the road, determined to end Lark's ordeal of having to sit beside him as soon as possible. He'd known she'd been hurt when things ended between them, but he'd always assumed she'd be happier without him. That she would move on faster since she was the one who'd decided to call it quits in the first place.

Now? He wondered if she'd recovered from their split any more than he had. He could have sworn he'd seen a hint of the old spark in her gaze when she'd first locked eyes with him today.

He'd felt the answering heat.

Fought the desire to act on it. For now, at least.

But his fierce competitive streak had helped drive him to the top of his career. And right now, that same hungry instinct hounded him to rekindle an old flame.

Two

The morning after her encounter with Gibson, Lark moved through the brightly tiled kitchen that had once belonged to her grandmother, flipping on the coffee-maker as she glanced outside the open window above the apron sink. The scent of late summer wildflowers filtered in on the warm breeze.

Dragging in deep breaths of fresh air, Lark told herself to enjoy the time here in her grandmother's house. This was real life, not whatever was happening online in the sports media world where she'd been photographed with Gibson the day before. Picking out the scents and sights of wild bergamot, fire-weed, blanket flowers and columbine, Lark used the grounding technique she often taught in counsel-ing sessions to calm her morning's anxieties about being back in the media spotlight, if only for the day. She'd also downloaded an app on her phone to try to minimize her exposure to social media, a trick she'd learned while still married to Gibson. She wouldn't get caught up in the old spirals of negative thinking that had always resulted from being married to an elite athlete.

She'd never thought for a moment that Gibson cheated on her, physically or romantically, but his energy had so often been focused on everyone around him, she felt overlooked at times.

Opening her eyes, Lark noticed out the window that Fleur's car was gone, which meant her chef sister was still at the Cowboy Kitchen, a local diner where she delivered fresh baked goods each morning. It was a way to earn money to finance Fleur's dream of opening a tapas place, and the Catamount community—small though it might be—had embraced Fleur's culinary skills. Now Fleur was doing local catering gigs too, preparing their Catalan grandmother's recipes and offering unique menus at weddings, birthday parties and other events.

When the coffee machine started to burble in earnest, Lark tugged open the old-fashioned refrigerator that contained bottle after bottle of goat's milk thanks to the three dairy goats Fleur kept. Bypassing these in favor of some soy milk she'd picked up at the store, Lark shut the fridge and poured herself a cup of coffee, the vibrant tiles echoing hollowly under her dishes.

The kitchen wasn't the same without Antonia Barclay. Back when Lark had been married to Gibson, and she'd helped him choose the house next door to this one for their off-season residence until he retired, she'd been so excited to spend more time in Catamount. She'd imagined shared summer afternoons with her grandmother at the very table where Lark carried her mug now to sit alone.

Then came the divorce, and she'd told herself she'd find another time to spend with Gran. And then, last spring, time ran out. Her chest ached at the knowledge that she wouldn't have another chance to visit with her warm, wise grandmother, the wave of sudden grief stronger than she would have expected after all these months...

The slam of a car door outside yanked her from the painful memories.

Voices followed. Happy laughter punctuating words she couldn't hear through the open window. Fleur had returned home with Jessamyn. For a moment, Lark wished she could join their easy conversation. She'd missed so much time with her sisters after their parents' bitter divorce had torn the family apart, requiring everyone to choose sides, a decision no child should have to make. It had been a no-brainer for Lark to choose their mother, Jennifer, since she'd done no wrong. Their father had been the one who'd cheated. But Jessamyn, for reasons known only to her, had always sided with their dad. Fleur, who on the surface had the most mild-mannered personality of the three of them, had been the only one to steadfastly refuse to choose, working double-time to maintain lines of communication with all, even when their father cut off financial assistance the moment she turned eighteen.

Lark had admired Fleur's stance, even though she'd never been tempted to mirror it. Their father was a self-absorbed asshat. End of story. Now that he was attempting to steal their inheritance from Antonia—the beautiful house and lands of Crooked Elm Ranch in Catamount—Jessamyn had left his company and Fleur had stopped trying to keep the peace.

The door burst open as Jessamyn strode inside, Fleur on her heels. They were both dressed in tennis shoes and denim cutoffs, a far cry from Jessamyn's usual clothes. As a New York City resident with a high-profile real estate job, Jessamyn normally wore designer everything. But maybe, now that she was transplanting herself to Catamount to make a life with Ryder, that would change. Funny how something simple like a change in clothes could make Lark see her sister differently, but it did. Maybe because the luxury wardrobe items had always reminded Lark that Jess had put her bank account over family.

"Big news!" Fleur squealed as she settled her burden of empty baking containers onto the counter near the sink. Fleur's copper-colored hair was tied in a ponytail, a pink scarf keeping the strands from her face. "You'll never guess what happened to Jessamyn."

Lark shifted her gaze to her other sister, walking into the house more slowly, her hands shoved in the back pockets of her shorts. Yet her face glowed with happiness even though she tried to suppress a smile.

"More big news?" Lark shook her head while she mused aloud, grateful to think about her sisters' lives rather than her own. At least Fleur and Jessamyn weren't talking about Gibson, or the damnable photos of Lark with her ex that were surely circulating online. "Let me think. Jessamyn's already knocked up. I don't think she'll top that for big news—" She stopped herself as a very real possibility came to mind. "Oh wow. Are you having twins?"

Fleur's laughter tripped through the kitchen. Jessamyn removed her left hand from her pocket and extended it for Lark to see.

Diamonds caught the morning sunlight, refracting tiny rainbows everywhere. A chevron shaped band pointed toward Jessamyn's fingertip, a cluster of diamonds surrounding the pear cut stone in the center.

Lark's focus went from the engagement ring to her sibling's face. The joy she saw there outshone any jewel. In that moment, Lark forgot all about their old enmity. She wanted to share her sibling's happiness. She even opened her mouth to congratulate Jess.

"I'm so happy for you—" she began, but her voice cracked with emotion that she had to clear her throat to hide. Memories of another ring lambasted her, along with all the hopeful optimism she'd felt when she'd said yes to Gibson. Would her regret over their lost bond ever stop hurting? Cursing herself—and her ex—she tried again. "For both of you."

The kitchen remained quiet for a moment, and as Jessamyn's smile dimmed a few shades, Lark sensed she hadn't been as effusive as the occasion called for.

She sort of hoped her sisters would write it off to her strained relationship with Jessamyn before they guessed the truth—that the failure of her own union still weighed heavily even after two years.

Forcing her lips into a smile, she poured soy milk into her coffee and made another effort. "So when's the date?"

"That's the other huge news," Fleur answered, drawing close to Jessamyn's side and sliding an arm around her shoulders in a squeeze.

A show of solidarity. Fleur was good like that.

"We're getting married in three weeks," Jessamyn announced, the brightness returning to her face, the happiness irrepressible.

And yeah, Lark remembered that feeling, too. Luckily, the time frame for a wedding was so ludicrous, it gave her something else to think about besides the endless optimism of new love.

"Three *weeks*?" Shaking her head, she stirred in the milk with her spoon while Fleur moved to the pantry and withdrew a dome-covered plate containing pastries visible through the clear glass. "Is it even possible to pull together a reception that quickly?"

Shrugging, Jessamyn reached into a cabinet to retrieve a bottle of prenatal vitamins and shook one into her hand. "We didn't want to wait with a baby on the way."

Fleur set the glass dish on the table and removed the dome with a flourish while Jessamyn brought over three plates. Lark eyed the almond croissants and slices of traditional Spanish sponge cake called *piononos*, but she already knew she'd choose the spiral pastry called *ensaimada de Mallorca*, one of her favorites their grandmother used to make.

Fleur had inherited the baking gene.

"I told her we'd help," Fleur added as she took a strategic seat between her siblings. She gave Lark a meaningful look. "They're going to have the reception here."

"At Crooked Elm?" Lark blinked in surprise, her hand pausing midway to the pastry she'd been reaching for. "Or do you mean here, as in Catamount?"

Jessamyn swiped the *ensaimada* Lark had been eyeing, spilling confectioners' sugar as she transferred it to her plate. "At Crooked Elm," she replied firmly. "Ryder offered to have it at Wakefield Ranch, but I've felt a strong pull to this place since I've been here. Besides, I think Gran would have loved a wedding here."

Loss echoed through her as Lark took a caramel and pecan *pionono*, memories of Gran vivid in her mind. Their grandmother was a practical woman, as down-to-earth as they came. She milked her own goats and grew her own vegetables, carving out a simple life here from the work of her own two hands. But she'd had a romantic side, especially where her granddaughters were concerned. They'd all seen photos of Antonia's backyard wedding where she'd taken her vows under an awning of honeysuckle. An errant pain stabbed at the thought of a future Lark would never have now that she'd ended her own marriage.

She blamed being back in Catamount for dredging up that hurt.

"That she would have," Lark admitted, recognizing she'd have to find a way to come to terms with her own negative feelings toward marriage so as not to mar her sister's day.

She'd promised Fleur she'd try, after all.

"Right?" Fleur chimed in cheerily. "Gran would have been all over this. So I think it will be a fun sister-bonding thing for the three of us to work on wedding planning a little each day, especially since we'll have some time now that the probate hearing is delayed."

Fun?

Lark suppressed a groan by gulping her coffee. She needed to figure out a way to get a handle on her feelings ASAP if she wanted to survive a day—no, *weeks*—of wedding planning. Potential excuses circled through her mind. A patient emergency in LA? Or she got called for jury duty? Contracted a contagious disease?

"It shouldn't be that big of an undertaking." Jessamyn licked sugar off her thumb between bites of pastry. "I mean, we can only do so much in three weeks anyway. I don't want the emphasis to be on a fancy gown or pricey party. What's important is sealing the deal with the man I love in front of our friends and family."

Lark's chest ached at the sentiment. A brief moment of superstition making her wonder if things hadn't worked out for her and Gibson because they'd done a courthouse wedding, circumventing the need to contend with complicated Barclay family politics. But of course, that wasn't the reason her marriage had crashed and burned. Gibson's travel and lack of commitment to a home life were to blame.

And, partly, Lark's inability to bridge the growing emotional gap his absences had created. The more charming he tried to be in those final months, the less she felt like he knew her at all. She'd craved reality, not the side he showed to the press.

"Aww," Fleur sighed happily at Jessamyn's words while Lark stuffed the final bite of pastry in her mouth in an effort to end this visit. "That's a beautiful idea, Jess, but we're going to do everything we can to make the day memorable, too. Aren't we, Lark?"

Fleur turned pleading gray eyes her way.

Mouth full, Lark nodded. Stretched her facial muscles into another semismile.

But this visit to Catamount now multiplied in difficulty by about one hundred. She'd thought it had been complicated by Gibson's presence in town. But now she had to contend with her ex next door all the while planning a wedding.

Salt? Meet wound.

Lifting aside the heavy plastic sheeting on the work site, Gibson toured the new addition on his house, taking note of the progress the builder had made over the past few days. The scent of freshly cut wood permeated the air as he stepped around a pile of white twelve-inch tiles delivered that morning.

The brick annex to the main structure of his home would be all on one floor, an addition that would make it easier for Gibson's mother to get around. Not that she was old. Stephanie Vaughn's physical body remained strong. Vigorous. It was cruel that early onset dementia was slowly stealing her mental health.

Gibson wandered into the bathroom, where the first walls to go up were the ones that would be tiled for a walk-in shower. There would be no step up, and no threshold, necessitating a large space to keep water off the rest of the floor. He wanted to make life as easy as possible for his mom, and for his mother's full-time caregiver. Yet he couldn't move either one of them to the house until the annex was complete. He lifted his phone to text his builder again and ask when he'd be onsite today.

It was a far better use of his time than scrolling through the photos of Lark and him that had started appearing online the day before, even though he couldn't help but see the picture again since he'd left a browser window open on the device.

Damn, but she still took his breath away.

The warmth of the day already filtered through the half-finished space, but he could hardly blame that for the rush of heat through his veins as his gaze swept over Lark's image, from her high cheekbones and forest-green eyes to the conservative clothes that never fully camouflaged the pinup-worthy body beneath.

Her shoulders were tense, her spine straight. Because of him? Or because of the media chasing them? He regretted bringing stress back into her life.

Gibson didn't know how much time elapsed while he stared at the photo, telling himself there was still a spark evident between them. But the next thing he knew, the device vibrated in his hand, a banner appearing across the photo with his agent's name for an incoming call.

Again.

Stifling an oath, he jabbed the button to connect them since he couldn't duck the guy forever. Better to get this conversation over with.

"Hey, Dex. What's up?" Gibson asked casually, moving out of the half-built annex and into the sunlight.

"Just wanted to let you know your stock is going up, my friend. The longer you stay silent on the rumors about your return to the ice, the more teams are wanting you. I had a third general manager call me this morning after your mug was all over the place online this morning."

"I'm retired. Remember?" It had been tough enough reaching the decision without the added pressure of his agent trying to keep him in the game. "I've remained silent on the subject because I've already made a public announcement about my retirement."

Dealing with his mother's illness had forced him to take a long look at his priorities. And he'd realized that he hadn't been paying enough attention to the people who were most important to him.

"Just until we get the right price for your comeback though," Dexter responded smoothly, ever-confident in his ability to negotiate terms. "I don't think you're going to find much to fill your days in that no-man's-land of a town you're living in after the excitement of professional hockey."

Gibson couldn't deny that he would miss playing. The ice had always been the one place in his life where he excelled—the one arena where he'd found success.

Unlike the failures of his personal life. The stress of his decision—knowing he'd have to fight hard every day to resist the temptation to return to his sport—combined with the worry over his mom's health and knowing that he'd upset Lark all over again, was a two-ton weight on his chest. He entered the garage from a side door to edge past his sports car and climb into his pickup truck.

He needed a break from the building site his home had become. A break from the media and the pressure of getting back in the game. He hit the button to open the garage door and started the truck's engine.

"I'm looking forward to some downtime," he reminded Dex, for what seemed like the tenth time, as he swapped the phone to Bluetooth through the vehicle's speakers.

He hadn't said much to his agent about the situation with his mom since, at the end of the day, they weren't really friends. Gibson respected Dex's business savvy, but he wasn't all that certain the guy had a life outside of sports.

Dexter spoke over the background noise of city streets, traffic and whistles, horns and air brakes. "You thought that once before though, remember?"

Of course he did. He'd been ready to retire to save his marriage. After a tough road trip through Canada, he'd told his agent he needed to retire, that the time had come to make his marriage a priority. But by the end of that playing season, Lark had already moved out of the home they shared. She'd packed up while he was on the road, not even bothering to inform him they were through until he found the last of her boxes in the foyer of their Los Angeles home.

He'd made the decision to retire a little too late, apparently. So he'd called Dex and told him not to schedule the retirement announcement. He'd played two more seasons until his mother's health worsened to the point where he couldn't ignore the decline.

"I remember all too well. But this time is different." Now his mom needed him.

Hell, Gibson had to prove to *himself* that he could be the son she needed. He'd messed up too many other things in his life to get this wrong.

Gibson backed out of the driveway just as his general contractor arrived for another's day work on the house addition. Gibson gave the guy a wave as they passed, then he stepped on the gas to head toward one of his favorite Catamount retreats, an old stone bridge that had fallen into disrepair along a backroad not far from his place.

Lark had taken him there once and they'd dangled their feet into the creek. He visited it often whenever he was in town now, always in hope of the peace they'd experienced there—together—that first time. Somehow, the spot was never quite the same without her, but that didn't stop him from returning there anyway.

"But the offers are only going to be available for so long, Gibson. You know that as well as I do." Dexter's warning felt more than a little ominous. "The clock is ticking."

Nothing like piling on the pressure.

Gibson nodded absently, even though his agent couldn't see him, as he drove along the feeder creek for the White River. The road had shade trees on either side, cooling the interior of his truck as they blocked the sun.

"I realize that, and I appreciate you looking out for me. But I don't see myself changing my mind about this." No matter how tough it would be to ignore all the texts from his teammates urging him to return for one more season, a year when a playoff run was finally a real possibility. Tough enough to ignore the social media stories from fellow players touting their off-season workouts.

Normally by this time of year, Gibson would be deep into endurance training to prepare for the fall, traditionally his favorite time of year.

Disconnecting the call on his dash, he planned to leave his phone in the truck cab once he reached the bridge. That way, he wouldn't be tempted to scroll.

And he wouldn't be distracted by any more photos of Lark.

Even though he was *sure* he'd seen signs of a spark between them in that picture that had run of them together. He was grateful when the bridge came into view up ahead since he needed some peace.

Except he wouldn't be finding it anytime too soon because he could see the tall, sexy figure of his ex-wife already there.

Three

Fingernails digging into the soft bark of a birch tree, Lark heard an approaching vehicle. Her breath hitched even before she turned to see her ex-husband's dust-covered blue pickup trundling along the bumpy road.

Had she come here—to a favorite spot of hers that she'd once shared with him—purposely hoping she might run into Gibson?

Of course not, she thought to herself as she turned back to the view of the shallow creek water rushing just below her feet. She was simply too stubborn to relinquish a spot she loved to him. She'd refused to take much from their marriage when they had ended things, recognizing that she'd brought little enough into the union with her very average salary and minimal belongings. But this? This quiet retreat place near the old bridge had been *hers* first.

Her spine stiffened at the sound of his truck door slamming. The crunch of his boots across dried leaves and pine needles on the forest floor.

Belly tightening as he approached, she forced out a long breath to calm the swell of emotion.

"I know I can't keep you from living in Catamount," she reminded him, lifting a stick from the ground to swipe through the surface of the creek. "But I don't think it's too much to ask if I want to claim this spot as my own."

Even her own ears could discern that she sounded more like a wounded child than a grown-ass woman. Why was it that this man could bring out the worst in her?

His step paused. Birds chirped and fluttered through tree branches overhead as Gibson went silent, giving her a moment to rethink her approach. A moment to regret. But before she could recant the inhospitable words, he spoke.

"You're right. It's not too much to ask." The timbre of his voice shot through her, the vibration of it familiar. Entwined with happy memories, not just sad ones. "Would you like me to go?"

Risking a glance at him, even knowing how appealing she always found him, Lark lifted her gaze from the creek bed.

Gibson stood some fifteen feet from her, dressed in jeans and a black T-shirt that outlined delineated muscles. His dark hair was still damp from a morning shower and combed away from his face.

"No. Forget I said that." She shook her head, remembering she was a licensed therapist and a professional woman, not an embittered former spouse. She could share the woods with this man for a few minutes, if only to show herself that she had moved on from Gibson Vaughn. "It's just been one of those weeks."

He nodded then continued toward her, his thighs flexing as he walked, straining the denim of his jeans as he moved. She'd forgotten that about him, how his body was more than just a thing of male beauty. It was a scrupulously maintained machine, a tool of his sport and one of the keys to being an elite athlete.

Her throat dried up as he reached her.

"Sit with me?" he asked, nodding toward the flat rock where they'd settled beside one another long ago.

She supposed it made sense to move past this enmity with him if they were going to see one another around town in the future. Besides, she didn't like what it said about her feelings that her back went up every time he was near. From a counseling perspective, she recognized the signs of unresolved issues.

"For a few minutes," she agreed, carefully setting a mental boundary for herself by referencing the time limit. Giving herself an out if she needed one.

Then, stepping out onto the ledge of a rock that had probably once served as a foundation for the long collapsed wooden bridge that had spanned the creek at one time, Lark lowered herself to the cool stone.

She wished she'd worn one of her long skirts today instead of the cotton shorts and tee she'd thrown on for a run earlier. From experience, she knew the more clothes between them the better if she wanted to hide her body's reaction to him.

Sometimes just the sound of his voice could give her goosebumps. His effect on her had always been so strong and at the same time, wildly unfair.

A point driven home as his knee brushed hers when he took the spot beside her. She tried not to skitter from him, but the effect of that touch, however innocuous, was potent.

But if Gibson noticed her struggle, he didn't remark on it. Instead, he leaned back on his hands and tipped his head to peer up at the canopy of trees overhead. A soft breeze fluttered the leaves in a continuous rustle, the scent of silty soil and dead leaves mingling with the pervasive smell of the pines.

"You once told me I should come out here when I needed space to breathe and think," he mused aloud. "I guess it's been one of those weeks for me, too."

Caught off guard that he recalled advice she'd given him—let alone that he still implemented it—Lark looked at him again. Really looked. Beyond the well-publicized physique and handsome face. There were shadows beneath his eyes, hints of sleepless nights and worries.

"Second-guessing retirement?" The old resentments crept in while a belted kingfisher sounded its rattling call.

While she waited for his answer, Lark glanced

up at the bird, its blue head and white neck feathers easily distinguished amid the green leaves of the birch. She hadn't meant to pick a fight with Gibson but damn it, his job had been impossible to live with. Or was it just his *commitment* to the job? His endless quest for excellence had consumed his time and energies, leaving him little leftover to share with her.

"Not second-guessing so much as wondering who to be now that I'm no longer a hockey player," he answered, not rising to the bait of an old argument. A self-deprecating smile lifted one side of his mouth before he finished drily, "An end-of-career identity crisis, I guess."

Was he truly concerned about that? It was a rare glimpse behind the composed, confident mask he usually showed to the world. But then, they'd met through her practice, before she'd switched her professional focus from sports psychology to counseling kids.

Gibson Vaughn had walked into her office one day for an initial consultation, but there'd been a spark between them immediately. She'd ignored it, of course, because she was a professional and that was a sacred line to her. But he'd refused to schedule a session with her, insisting he wanted a date instead.

She'd never been more grateful for a canceled appointment in her life.

After a few weeks of getting to know one another through texts and phone calls, she'd agreed to come to an afternoon game and dinner with him afterward. He wasn't merely charming and attractive; he'd been persistent. Focused on her completely. And he hadn't given up once he'd made up his mind. What woman could resist that brand of wooing? She'd been swept off her feet.

And she was not a woman to get carried away by romance. Until Gibson, she hadn't even believed it existed. The memories of her broken family had made her distrustful of relationships. She'd had to become so independent that she had trouble being vulnerable to anyone. Gibson had broken through the first layers, but they hadn't had enough time together to work through all her issues.

"So you're going to turn your property into a working ranch?" She watched the kingfisher leave its branch to dive headfirst into the creek, coming up a moment later with a pale colored fish in its long beak. "My grandmother mentioned that's what you were planning the last time I spoke to her."

When he didn't respond right away, Lark pulled off her shoes to dip a toe in the water while she turned to observe him. He had straightened in his seat to pick a blade of grass from a crack in the rock.

"Antonia told me I had all the makings of a good rancher."

The warmth in his voice reminded Lark how much Gibson had enjoyed her grandmother. He'd said his family had never been close, but it was a subject he never lingered on. She'd gotten the impression his dad had been the stern, withholding sort before he'd left the family when Gibson was eight or nine.

After that, his mother had worked two jobs to support herself and her son, making interactions between them infrequent. Lark had liked Stephanie Vaughn a great deal and sensed she wanted to be closer with her son, but Gibson seemed to keep her at a distance.

Now, Lark's defenses crumbled at his regard for her loved one. She was grateful for the creek water flowing around her feet, the cool chill keeping a check on her emotions.

"If Gran said it, then it must be true." She watched as he wound the grass blade around one long finger, his hands crisscrossed with old scars. "But you'd be good at a lot of things. What's more important is to find something you'll enjoy."

He gave a mirthless laugh, the grass falling forgotten through his fingers. "I enjoy things that I'm good at."

The idea scratched at an old memory she couldn't quite call to the surface, the notion bothering her. She dug her toes into the silty earth beneath the water.

"Gibson, you're at a fortunate place in life financially that some people never achieve. You could follow any dream you're passionate about—"

"Not true," he corrected her, shifting to face her. Behind him, the eroded bridge pilings made a moss-covered backdrop. "I was passionate about you once, Lark. That's a dream I'll never have back."

Her thoughts evaporated like mist, the draw of this man compelling even after all the heartache he'd caused her. But she knew better than to act on it now, no matter how much he affected her. He hadn't fought for her, she reminded herself. Not even a little bit.

She wouldn't have ever asked him to retire, but she felt sure he could have found ways to be home more between road trips. Other players did. And he could have found ways to help ease her sense of loneliness and disconnect when they were apart.

"Giving up on that dream was a choice we both made." Shaking her head, she flicked her toes along the surface of the creek, sending a spray onto a nearby log. "Now, what happened with us is sort of like this…" She kicked up another small spray, startling a bullfrog on the shore. "Water under a fallen down, forgotten bridge."

Which reminded her that they really weren't going to resolve any of the old issues between them today, no matter how much she wished that seeing him didn't affect her. So, getting to her feet, she slid on her shoes again and told herself this was a good time to walk away.

Gibson let her words rattle around his head for a moment as Lark strode away from him. Retreating. He wanted to call to her, but he also recognized the need for caution in his response.

He disagreed with her. Strongly.

But he knew better than to cross swords with his clever ex-wife unless he was truly ready to dig in and stand by what he said. Her experience as a counselor made it easy for her to see through bullshit and ego. She had a way of carving right to the deeper point of an argument, even before he realized what they were arguing about.

So he weighed and considered. Chewed on the idea of their old dreams being forgotten. Water under the proverbial bridge.

And still couldn't let her indictment of their past slide. He couldn't let her pretend their time together was all bad, that it meant nothing. Shooting to his feet, he jogged a few steps along the creek toward the path that led to Crooked Elm, catching up to her quickly.

"You have to know that's not true, Lark."

"Which part?" She swung around to face him, green eyes brighter than usual, the color of spring moss. "Us both giving up on the dream? Or that our past is over and forgotten?"

Inside, his brain insisted that he hadn't been the one to give up on the dreams they shared, even though he'd moved on since then, damn it. But his sixth sense told him that was dangerous terrain for an argument. Instead, he stuck with the safer view.

They stood close now. Nearer to one another than they'd been on the rock ledge. He caught a hint of her fragrance—the lavender soap she preferred and some kind of minty shampoo she used. Nostalgia slammed him, almost as strong as the jolt of desire that was automatic whenever she was near him.

"Our past may be over, but clearly neither of us have forgotten it. Otherwise, seeing each other wouldn't be so—" His gaze dipped from her eyes to…lower. All without his permission. He forced his attention back up where it belonged even as his fingers flexed with the urge to touch her. "—*charged*."

Her lashes flicked briefly. Hardly a flutter. But definitely a sign that she'd needed a moment to collect herself.

"That has more to do with wounded pride than anything else." She tilted her chin at him, a silent dare to contradict her. "I don't think either of us enjoy failing at something we set out to accomplish."

"Is that what you think our marriage was? A failure?" And damn, but she knew how to push his buttons.

"It ended in a courthouse with you going one way and me going another." Her eyes flashed, breath quickening. "What else can we possibly label it?"

Two great years where he got to call her his wife. Then she'd walked away from him when he needed her most. But he'd be damned if he'd revisit that hurt now.

"Call it what you like. You can't deny the pull between us even now. You can file all the dissolution of marriage papers you want, but you can't dissolve attraction with a court order."

She opened her mouth, presumably to argue with him, then snapped it shut again. Clamped her teeth in her lower lip for good measure.

He felt the light scrape of those straight white teeth in his mind's eye, a phantom, teasing brush of them along his shoulder. His abs. And lower.

Yeah, the attraction hadn't gone anywhere.

His thoughts must have shown in his eyes because a slight shiver went through her, so subtle he would have missed it if he'd blinked. They stood together, breathing in the same air as the space between them seemed to shrink. His hands lifted, very ready to touch her.

Until a bird streaked past them, plunging into the creek with a splash.

Lark startled away from him, seeming to recover herself as she resurrected some space between them. Disappointment swelled even as he knew he should be grateful for the interruption. He didn't have a plan where Lark was concerned, and his record with her had proven that wasn't wise.

But it didn't make him want her any less.

"Just because an attraction exists doesn't mean we have to act on it." She tugged at the shirt cuffs on her long-sleeved tee, as if covering up as much skin as possible would somehow mitigate the chemistry. "We're adults. And obviously, we know better now."

Above the trees, the sun must have dipped behind some clouds, casting them in sudden shadow.

"You keep telling yourself that." He took a step back, dragging in a calming breath. "In the meantime, I wanted to see if there's anything I can do to help with your case against your father."

His swift change of subject was purposeful. He needed a distraction if he wanted to stop thinking about touching Lark.

And he'd been incensed on her behalf when he'd heard her dad was contesting Antonia's will. News traveled fast in a small town like Catamount. His other neighbors had been quick to fill him in on the local drama.

"I appreciate that." She regarded him with new interest. Curiosity. "But I'm not sure there's anything you can do unless Antonia articulated her plans for Crooked Elm with you."

An errant birch leaf floated down to rest on Lark's shoulder briefly before she shrugged it away, her focus staying firmly on him.

"She absolutely did. She told me more than once that she was planning to leave the house and lands to you and your sisters." He'd spent quite a few happy hours with the older woman, helping her with the goats or dropping off grocery items after a run to the store.

At first, he'd done those things to be neighborly, but in a short space of time he found himself over at Crooked Elm just for the enjoyment of talking to the wise and witty older lady. She had an opinion about everything and wasn't afraid to share it, but she also wasn't the kind of person who tried to convert him to her way of thinking. She embraced the "live and let live" school of thought, content to let those around her walk their own path. It made her easy to talk to.

"Really?" Lark clamped a hand around his wrist, her fingers cool against his bare skin. "Gran said that to you? In those words?"

Gibson's heart thudded harder in reply to the touch. Responding to her nearness.

"She said as much in many different ways. Before you and I divorced, your grandmother frequently alluded to the time when you could join your portion of her lands with mine. It made her happy to envision you here in Catamount full-time." As he shared the memory, he noticed Lark's face clouded. "But even afterward, when you and I split, she still talked about how you'd come home one day, even if it was just to sell your share of Crooked Elm."

He hadn't liked thinking about that. About Lark walking away from a place she'd loved visiting as a kid. She'd adored it when they were married, sharing her pleasure in the place with him so that he'd been eager to buy a home for them here.

Now, she released his wrist abruptly as if she'd just recalled they were touching. Her tongue darted around the rim of her lips before speaking. "That would be really valuable testimony if you were willing to share an official statement with the court."

His gaze remained fixed on her mouth, his thoughts wildly inappropriate. He nodded at first, his throat too dry to speak. Then, forcing the words, he managed, "Of course I will."

"Great. Thank you." She danced back a step, making him wonder if the pull between them was as electric for her as it felt for him. "Fleur and Jessamyn will be thrilled to hear it, too."

Her feet continued to shuffle away, shifting the pine needles and leaves as she moved. And seeing her careful avoidance made him realize all at once that he needed the leverage this good turn could earn him.

"Wait." He hated to be that guy who traded on doing the right thing. But damn it, Lark wasn't going to give him the time of day if he didn't use this as a way to see her again. "Can I ask a favor in return?"

She arched an eyebrow. "If the gratitude of my family isn't rewarding enough for you, I guess you may."

For a moment, he was tempted to ask for something selfish. A kiss. A date. A chance to see that gorgeous hair of hers falling down around her naked shoulders one more time. Any of those things would be easier to request than what he really had in mind.

"I hoped you might stop by to see my mother the next time she's at the house, Lark. Not for long. Just for a quick hello." He saw the surprise in her eyes. Sympathy, even. So she did remember his mom's diagnosis. But he couldn't think about that—about his ex-wife doing anything for them out of sympathy—or he'd lose his nerve to ask for this boon. "She speaks of you often."

He didn't mention that his mother inquired every single time she saw him. Multiple times, thanks to the early onset dementia. He'd given up trying to remind her what had happened between him and Lark. It was too tough to recount that painful time in his life over and over again.

"Oh. How kind of her." Lark nodded quickly, agreeing. "I'll definitely do that. Just let me know next time she's around."

"Will do." Bargain struck, Gibson backed up a step, hoping it hadn't been a mistake to ask. "And if you put me in touch with your attorney, I'll work on that statement for you."

"I'll text you the contact information." She seemed flustered, which was unusual for Lark. "Thanks again for offering to help with the case."

At his nod, she pivoted fast, making tracks along the path that would follow the creek to the Crooked Elm Ranch. Gibson watched her go, eyes following her every step, wondering if it would ever get easier to see this woman walk away from him.

Four

"Lark, you're just in time!" Fleur waved from the backyard.

Two days had passed since Jessamyn's engagement announcement, and the house was routinely in an uproar with wedding plans. Lark had tried to be a good sport about it even though she and Jessamyn hadn't spoken much in years. But morning, noon and night there had been talk of dresses, possible attendants, a registry, food for the reception and a million and one other details.

Until she'd been ready to pull her hair out by the roots.

Instead, Lark had locked herself in the dining room at Crooked Elm for a few hours of telehealth visits with her patients back in Los Angeles, but she'd only stepped out of the house for a breath of fresh air and already her sisters were flagging her down. Fleur stood by the picnic table with the future bride and groom. A Bluetooth speaker sat on one bench, playing a classical piece of music.

Her wedding radar clicked into high alert.

"I'm only out here for a few minutes though." Lark hesitated as she stepped off the back porch onto the grass. The sun was low on the horizon, casting a mellow pink and orange glow over the surrounding fields. "I still need to finish up some paperwork before I can call it a day."

The bane of her existence as a counselor: the reports she needed to file seemed endless sometimes.

"This will only take a second," Fleur promised, gesturing to the engaged couple beside her who were staring deeply into one another's eyes, all smiles. "Jessamyn wanted me to show her and Ryder how to waltz, and it will be easier if I have a partner."

Lark's gaze stuck on Jessamyn. Dressed in a denim miniskirt and black T-shirt with the name of a local rodeo, her sister looked like she been born and raised on a ranch, right down to the dusty turquoise cowboy boots she wore. Jess had one hand on Ryder's shoulder, the other curved around his palm, while the local search and rescue hero stared into her eyes as if she were the only woman in the world. And maybe she was, for him.

The obvious love made Lark think of her own wedding. Gibson had stared at her once just that way, and she remembered exactly how it had made her feel inside. As if she was the luckiest woman on earth. As if their love were so deep and true it would pull them through any hardship life had to offer.

Until it hadn't.

Her throat burned so badly that she needed to swallow before she answered. "I don't know how either," she began, not wanting any part of dancing lessons.

"I'll teach you, too," Fleur insisted, lacing her fingers together to pantomime begging. "Please? I need a warm body to be my partner."

Seeing no way to refuse gracefully, Lark joined them. Fleur had wanted this time together in Catamount to repair their sister bond, but she hadn't said anything about subjecting Lark to daily doses of wedding mania. From the dinnertime discussions about writing your own vows to the breakfast chats about honeymoon clothes, being in the house with her sisters this week had rubbed her emotions raw. But she didn't want them looking too deeply into her aversion to all things matrimonial.

"Okay. What do I do?" Edgy and uncomfortable, Lark forced her attention to stay fixed on Fleur while she cued up a new song on her phone.

A familiar country ballad began, the romantic lyrics scraping over Lark's skin like sandpaper while Fleur moved toward her.

"It's simple really. We'll do a country waltz since you'll have The Haymakers playing at the reception." Fleur grinned at this, still thrilled that she'd booked the popular Western band last minute because they'd had a cancellation in their schedule. "This song is on their suggested playlist for ranch weddings."

"I love this one." Jessamyn practically swooned into Ryder as she said it.

Not that Lark was watching them. Gritting her teeth, she willed Fleur to get on with the lesson so she could stop thinking about how it felt to be wildly, hopelessly in love. Lark had already given Gibson way too much space in her head today, his image filling her phone screen as she scrolled through social media. It didn't matter that she'd blocked the sports news outlets. All her local friends and nearby small businesses seemed to be buzzing about the question of Gibson Vaughn's retirement. Everyone had an opinion about whether or not he would settle in Catamount to start ranching this time, or if he'd return to another hockey team before the season began.

There'd even been a few old photos of the two of them together, images that had made her shut down her phone for the day. Who knew she'd bounce from reminders of her failed marriage to dancing lessons beside the world's happiest couple?

"So what next?" she prompted Fleur, while the Nubian goats that had belonged to their grandmother made a ruckus in their pen nearby.

The goats were adorable with their long ears and playful ways, but they were definitely vocal, bleating to one another and to the backyard dancers.

Fleur removed the flour-dusted apron she'd been wearing around a pair of yellow overalls, then tossed it on the picnic table before she answered.

"Well, the country waltz is in three-quarter time, the same as the American waltz. Just listen for it." Fleur hummed along with the tune for a few moments, exaggerating the "One, two, three" count so the rest of them could hear it.

Lark focused on the rhythm, telling herself the sooner she conquered the steps, the faster she could be released from the day's romance session.

"Now, let's get into our dance positions." Fleur flipped her copper-colored ponytail behind her and moved closer to Lark, laying a hand on her waist. "Ryder and I will lead, Jess and Lark, you'll follow so your first step is backward on the count of one."

She demonstrated the basic steps and Lark mirrored her, an unexpected memory drifting up from her childhood. She'd danced like this once. Not at her own wedding of course, since she and Gibson had opted for fast and private over a public declaration of their vows.

There'd been a time…before her parents' bitter split. Before all the family fractures that had followed. Beneath all those rifts, there'd been happy times. Her singing along with the radio in the kitchen of her girlhood home. It had been a warm summer morning, and her father swooped her into his arms, standing her on his feet to dance her across the tile floor.

He'd still been her hero then. Back when she'd believed he'd been a good person.

She missed a step, stumbling on Fleur's toes.

"I'm sorry." Righting herself, Lark let go of her sister. "I probably shouldn't do this while I'm distracted by—" she cleared her throat as she produced an excuse "—my work."

What did she even do with a memory like that? She'd spent too long resenting her father—for good reason—to dwell on any redeeming qualities he might have once had. He'd turned his back on his family, not her.

"Is anything wrong?" Fleur asked, her gray eyes keen as she studied her.

At the same time, Jessamyn whirled past them in Ryder's arms, still dipping and stepping to a one-two-three count. "It's all good! I think we've got it down well enough to survive our couples dance."

This time, Lark was grateful for her sibling's starry-eyed romance since it distracted Fleur from inquiring more about what troubled her.

"I really should return to work." Lark edged away another step, seeing her chance to escape.

Between the constant reminders of her ex-husband next door, the pheromone-filled atmosphere at Crooked Elm with both her sisters in love and the pending court case with her father, she felt pushed to her personal breaking point this week.

"If you really have to," Fleur said reluctantly, moving toward the animal enclosure to scratch a friendly black-and-white goat named Guinevere. "But can you check in with Mom sometime tonight to ask for her flight details? I know she's booked her trip here for the wedding, and it would be great if you could pick her up at the airport."

"Really?" she blurted before realizing how rude

she sounded. She moved closer to Fleur to scratch one of the other goats—was the brown and white one Morgan Le Fay?—who headbutted her in the hip. "I mean, of course I'll find out when she's flying and I can take care of the airport run. I'm just surprised she agreed to come to Catamount…" Lark's gaze found Jessamyn where she still twirled and laughed with Ryder as they worked on their waltz moves. "Er—while the court case is in progress."

She was actually sort of surprised Mom had signed on for the wedding in the first place given the way Jessamyn had taken their dad's side in the split. While Mom had never held that against Jess, Lark knew their relationship had been strained. Diplomatic avoidance had been their usual MO.

Fleur glanced toward the dancing couple too, following Lark's attention.

"Well for starters, Jessamyn reached out to Mom after she got engaged and it sounds like they had a good talk." Fleur straightened the blue collar around Guinevere's neck with a silver name tag in the shape of a crown—a recent gift from Drake. "And once they started discussing the will contest case, it turns out Mom had a lot of ideas for potential witnesses who heard Gran talk about leaving Crooked Elm to us. Including Mom."

Lark's hand stilled on Morgan le Fay's neck. "You don't think Mom wants to get involved in the case? I mean, I'm all for winning this thing, but do any of us really want to see Mom and He-Who-Shall-Not-Be-Named facing off in another courtroom battle?"

Their family had barely survived the first one.

She'd begun her college studies in psychology at first, not because she'd had her heart set on being a therapist, but in order to have a reasoned, rational approach to analyzing what had gone wrong in her family. It had been her way of coping with a hurt that was, in essence, an abandonment. One day, she'd known two loving parents. Then her mother caught her father cheating and Lark found her own home a war zone with both the adults too consumed with their anger to remember things like after-school pickups, sports practices, or to even buy groceries. One of their money arguments turned into a contest to see who could go the longest without being the one to make a supermarket run.

At sixteen years old, Lark became the one to bum rides from friends who could drive in order to obtain food for the week with her babysitting money. Later in life, she'd learned about her mom's depression and had been able to forgive her for those dark months that had turned into two torturous years. But understanding those times hadn't made them easier to survive while she'd been going through them.

Fleur shrugged, her attention shifting to a stretch of backroad leading to Crooked Elm that was visible from this corner of the yard, where a dust cloud stirred in the dry air. "Mom is in a good, healthy place now. I think it should be her call. Besides, the attorney is accepting written statements, not just in-person testimonies."

Lark didn't share her easy acceptance of the idea.

In fact, her stomach tightened into a knot. "Written statements that could easily lead to in-person testimony if the judge wants more information, or if Dad's attorney wants to question any of them."

This week was tough enough with Gibson in town and facing her manipulative, self-centered father. She wasn't ready to relive the toxic family dynamics, too.

"It will be fine." Fleur's tone was placating at best as she still stared out toward the road. Distracted. "I don't recognize that vehicle coming toward us. Do you?"

Sighing at the way Fleur wasn't taking her concern seriously, Lark took a sidestep to see around a low hanging branch of a cottonwood tree.

Could it be Gibson? Her heart did a funny quickening that she firmly ignored. But the SUV moving through the dust cloud sure wasn't Gibson's truck or his sports car, both of which Fleur probably would recognize since he'd started spending more time at his house just a stone's throw from Crooked Elm.

Although he would use that road to approach the house. There weren't many places to access the quiet country lane, and Gibson's home—the one they were supposed to have shared—was one of them.

"I'm not sure." Lark took a few more steps toward the tree line that hid some of the thoroughfare, squinting to see through the dirt kicked up by the vehicle.

"I think there's a logo on the side—" Fleur began at the same exact moment Lark recognized it.

"It's the pain-in-my-ass sports media," she muttered, the knot in her stomach tightening as she headed for the back door. "And there's no way I'm letting them take pictures so they can use me for their stupid clickbait headlines."

She could already see it: "Where Are They Now? Former Hockey Wives We Loved to Hate."

At least they hadn't filmed her country waltzing in the yard with the goats as a backdrop. They'd try to fabricate a story about how lonely she was without Gibson in her life that she needed to dance alone. That's all her family needed was an excuse to probe.

Angry at the whole pseudo-industry that was loosely labeled sports entertainment "media" and didn't have a damned thing to do with news or even *sports*, Lark slowed her step.

Why should she have to hide herself away just because she resented them so much? Did it really matter what they had to say anymore now that her marriage was already over?

She'd come to Catamount to put the past behind her, after all. To bury the hatchet with her sisters. To secure Crooked Elm from her father's greedy clutches. And, most recently, to heal her guilt about her part in a failed marriage.

Maybe it was high time she gave the proverbial middle finger to her old enemy, the sports media, too. How long was she going to allow them to write her script for her, while she ducked and hid and hoped they wouldn't notice her? How had she let herself become that woman?

She had things to say for herself, damn it. Why

not use the platform rather than run from it, at least this one time?

"You can go inside," Fleur urged her as they heard the SUV tires on the gravel driveway in front of the house. "We'll make sure they know they have to stay off the property."

Shaking her head, Lark rolled up her sleeves, preparing for a showdown.

"There's no need. They want a story? It's long past time I gave them a good one."

Gibson was in the middle of a teleconference meeting with his newly hired ranch manager when his phone vibrated for the third time in a row. And even though he hadn't begun true ranch operations yet, the meeting was important if he ever wanted to get his new business off the ground.

He'd carefully researched the market for a bison ranch and found a good opportunity for profit. Plus, he admired the majestic beasts and looked forward to working with them.

"Will you excuse me for a minute?" he asked the new hire as he leaned back from the workspace he'd set up at the dining room table.

With so much of the house under construction to be comfortable for his mother's arrival, Gibson hadn't bothered to furnish much of the upstairs, preferring to wait until the dust settled on the renovations.

"Sure thing," Jackson Daly tipped the brim of his Stetson at him on the other end of the video call.

"Though I've got enough to keep me busy until next week's meeting."

"Sounds good to me." Gibson had requested revenue projections for the business plan he was putting together for a few friends who had expressed interest in investing. "Thanks, Jackson."

After closing out of the app on his laptop screen, Gibson pressed the connect button on the call from—surprise, surprise—his agent.

Again.

"Dex, I'm still committed to starting the ranch." He told himself as much every day, even though the project had a huge chance of flopping.

If he ever wanted to conquer the fear of failure—of losing—he couldn't spend his whole life only taking on things that he was good at.

"Are you watching the news?" Dex blurted, his voice sounding tenser than normal. Gibson could hear a phone ringing along with what sounded like multiple news feeds running in the background.

A sea of talking heads.

"Of course not. I'm working, and even if I weren't…" Gibson leaned far back in the ergonomic desk chair he'd bought for his long frame, tilting the neck rest so he stared up at the sleek chrome light fixture hanging over the blond wood table. "You know I didn't check out the sports headlines even when I was playing—"

"Not the sports news. Turn on your local network affiliate. They've been promoting the hell out of a story with a clip of your ex-wife. It'll be on as soon as they return from commercial."

Gibson tipped forward so quickly he nearly fell out of the chair. "They're back to chasing Lark around town?"

Pounding one fist on the table, he used his other to reach for the television remote that controlled a big screen across the great room above the fireplace. He cursed the media hounds the whole time for interfering in his personal life again, after he'd made some progress with Lark.

"From the sound bite they keep showing, it sure didn't look like she was trying to avoid them this time." Dex's words sounded muffled, as if he were covering the phone or maybe sandwiching it between his chin and shoulder. The guy juggled too much, but for once, Gibson appreciated the heads-up considering he was to blame for bringing the spotlight with him to Catamount.

Jabbing a few buttons to find the right channel, Gibson blasted the volume on the remote in time to see Lark's pretty face fill the television screen. Her sexy dark braid lay coiled on one shoulder bared by a white tank dress as she stood in front of the Crooked Elm Ranch house. Her expression was serious as she looked directly into the camera.

"…because since when does reporting on the activities of elite athletes' wives, girlfriends and exes constitute sports news?" Lark had taken the microphone out of the hand of whoever had been trying to interview her. She moved backward now as someone reached into the frame to try to retrieve it. Lark's forest-green eyes flashed with a fire Gibson remembered well from their arguments. And from other times...

She continued now, "If you're going to cover women, why not give camera time to actual women athletes who are overlooked by the media and paid far less than their male counterparts?"

The camera work turned awkward then, the lens bouncing as whoever carried the video recorder moved to forcibly take the mic out of Lark's hands. But not before Lark could be heard saying, "Do you know how many professional women's teams there are in Los Angeles where I live? And do you know how many more times I made your stupid news feed over talented, trained women who deserve—"

The video and audio ended abruptly, the local anchor appearing on the screen with a still image from the clip behind one shoulder labeled "Gibson Vaughn's Ex Speaks Out."

Indignation on her behalf fired through him. They couldn't even give her the credit of her own name under her photo? But the local anchor moved quickly to another story, leaving Gibson to wonder when— and how—they'd obtained a clip that clearly hadn't been shot by their own team.

More than that, his thoughts were at Crooked Elm with Lark. Was she upset about the encounter? Pleased? She'd definitely taken the offensive this time, and he couldn't be prouder of her about that. He remembered too well how frustrated the media had made her when they'd been married.

"Good for her," Gibson mused aloud, almost forgetting he had Dex on the phone in the onslaught of thoughts about Lark. She'd looked sexy as hell in that clip. "Thanks for the heads-up about this."

"I didn't call just to give you a heads-up." Again, a phone rang in the background of wherever Dex was sitting, a racket all around the guy. "I'm getting bombarded with opportunities for you. Teams that think you must be considering a comeback if Lark is putting herself in the spotlight."

Shoulders slumping, Gibson didn't know what to say to that other than that tired old refrain. "Not going to happen."

He would have pounded home the point except a notification from the security guard at his front gate chimed on his phone. Pulling it from his ear, he read the message.

Lark is out front. Should I let her through?

Surprise made him hesitate for only an instant. Then he tapped an auto-response command in the affirmative. Damn right he wanted to see her, even if he couldn't imagine what she was doing here.

Returning his phone to his ear as he rose to his feet, he strode to the door while Dex continued speaking without pause. "And there are two new teams interested in you because of this new attention. A lot of hockey clubs are trying to be supportive of women's teams and this really resonates—"

Clearly he hadn't missed much of the conversation. His agent was giving the same old spiel while headlights arced across Gibson's windows. Anticipation thrummed through him.

Gibson pulled open the front door as Lark herself stepped from a gray sedan, her long legs encased in fitted black boots. She still wore the same white tank dress she'd had on in the television clip.

And she was here. At his house.

Making him want her simply by being.

His throat was dry when he spoke again. "Dex, I have to go now. I'll call later. Bye."

Shutting the phone off and tossing it on the couch and well out of reach, Gibson held the door open wide for his too-gorgeous ex-wife who'd just set him on fire with her take-no-prisoners approach with the media.

Whatever she wanted, he was more than happy to provide.

Five

Lark's thoughts scrambled at the sight of her ex-husband on his front doorstep. The overhead porch light cast his chiseled features in shadow, his broad shoulders and strong chest stretching the fabric of a blue dress shirt with the sleeves rolled up and the top buttons unfastened. Dark gray trousers hugged his thighs, while his sock-clad feet padded onto the painted black floor of the deep porch.

Seeing him there, looking tousled after a work-day, reminded her of other homecomings when they'd lived together. On his rare days off when he'd cooked for her, he would greet her this way, the scents of a simple roasted chicken or grilled steaks drifting out the door while he wrapped her in those massive arms. Just thinking about it made her gaze return to them now, the musculature so well-defined he could have been an anatomy diagram. A very hot diagram.

"This is a welcome surprise." His voice jarred her from thoughts she had no business thinking. "Will you come in?"

Shaking off the hunger that seemed to grow every time she saw him, Lark flipped her braid behind her shoulder and took a step forward. She'd driven over here, after all. She couldn't pretend it had been an accident.

She'd expected to see the media camped outside his gates, but there'd been no one there except the security guard. Perhaps the local cops flushed out unwanted visitors now and then. Whatever the reason, she needed a safe haven from reporters.

Yet setting foot inside Gibson's house with him looking at her the way he was right now would only lead to her making questionable decisions.

"That's not necessary but thank you." She folded her arms across her chest, gathering her defenses against all six feet four inches of male charisma staring back at her.

He lifted one dark eyebrow in question. "It may not be necessary, but I think we'd be more comfortable if we took a seat while you tell me what brought you over here."

Glancing around the front yard of the home they'd chosen together, Lark tried to find a good reason to remain out of doors.

"It's such a nice night though," she hedged, her heart thumping too hard, too fast. "Maybe we could sit on the porch swing? That is, if you still have it hanging up on the back side of the house?"

Already she felt foolish for driving here, of all places, when she'd been agitated from the media interview and her emotions were already scraped raw from romantic dances in her backyard. But she hadn't been able to think of anywhere else to take shelter until she was certain the reporters were gone.

"Sure thing." Nodding, Gibson waved her around to the rear of the place, leading her along the polished floor planks. "It's a good spot for watching sunsets, just like we guessed it would be."

They'd been excited to purchase the property. So hopeful that it would help heal the growing rift between them created by his long absences. But there'd been one delay after another with the sale, and in the end, they hadn't been able to hang on long enough to see if the house could be a magic elixir to fix their broken relationship.

Frustration over all that they'd lost—so much more than Gibson knew—put the starch in her spine that she needed for this visit.

"I'm glad you're enjoying this part of the estate at least." She followed him around the house to the veranda in back where a low half-moon illuminated the cedar swing painted gray. "I noticed you're renovating most of the rest of it."

Taking a seat on the far end of the swing, she regretted commenting on the home as soon as the words were out of her mouth. It didn't matter what changes he made to his house. The property was no concern of hers anymore.

Even if a tiny, ugly part of her brain wondered if there was a girlfriend behind the redesign of a perfectly good residence.

"I'm adding a suite for Mom," he told her simply, tossing aside a plump ivory-colored throw pillow before he lowered himself into the swing. "So I've been grateful for a few places to retreat from the dust of remodeling."

Surprised at the big undertaking for the mother he didn't see often, Lark regretted her snarky thoughts. The starch in her spine wilted again as she watched Gibson stretch his long legs, one knee splayed so it rested inches from her own.

"That's good of you." Tugging another throw pillow out from behind her back, she hugged it in front of her instead. If she kept her hands gripping the cushion, she couldn't possibly reach out to touch him. "And sorry to show up here unannounced. I had a run in with the media—"

"I saw you go on the offensive." A wide grin stole over his features, white teeth glinting in the moonlight. "That was so freaking perfect."

"That clip is already online?" She knew video snippets like that circulated fast, but that had to set a new record. "I only lost the last of the reporters half an hour ago. I was afraid they would be waiting for me at Crooked Elm and I didn't know where else to go."

And how messed up was it that the first place she thought of to duck the press was with Gibson? He'd been the one to bring them back to her doorstep to begin with.

"Wait. Someone was following you? Not the asshat who interviewed you in the first place." His brow furrowed as he shifted to face her, his voice indignant. "The guy stole your mic just when you got going—"

Confused, she shook her head. "No. He retreated to his van after that. But there was a young woman filming from an unmarked car that pulled into Crooked Elm after the first guy. I have no idea who she worked for or how she knew to show up just then."

The members of entertainment media were like bees that way. One member of the hive could spot something juicy and minutes later, a swarm amassed.

"Probably a freelancer hoping for a toe in at one of the big media outlets." Gibson shook his head, his dark hair brushing his shoulders as he splayed his arms wide in a helpless gesture. "Although how anyone rationalizes stalking people for a living is sickening. Are you okay?"

His warm hand landed on her bare shoulder. A gesture of concern. Comfort, even.

Yet given how long it had been since they'd touched, the physical contact overrode her senses and short-circuited her brain. She couldn't think. Couldn't recall what he'd just said.

There was simply his hand. Touching her.

Lark's heartbeat redoubled. Squeezing the pillow tighter, she willed herself to speak.

"This was a mistake." Bolting upright from the seat, she took two long strides away from him, the swing's chains jangling softly in her wake. "I should go home now."

"Lark?" Soft concern laced Gibson's voice as he rose to follow her. "What's wrong? Did something happen with the press that we should report? Because if they crossed a line—"

He left the sentence half-finished as his gaze roved over her, as if checking to be sure she was still in one piece.

Old angers simmered anew, a welcome outlet for the fire still heating her blood from just a single touch of this man's hand.

"Where exactly is the line these days anyway, Gibson? I'm not sure I'd have any idea what violates my privacy when you assured me that having cameras camped out around my garage every time you were in the headlines was normal." Her fingers gripped the swing cushion so tight her fingernail popped off some of the beading near a tassel.

She slapped the silk-covered pillow onto a nearby table, frustrated at herself for letting her emotions get the best of her. For permitting the smallest caress to overwhelm her.

"They're not allowed to touch you. They're not allowed to block your way," he repeated the guidelines she remembered well, his tone betraying his own agitation. "You know that."

"Whereas speculating on our love life, asking me loaded questions to imply you were unfaithful to me every time you were on the road, and goading me to speak until they had a juicy sound bite, that's all just fine." Lark knew she needed to rein it in.

Her words were far too revealing. Not just to him, but even to herself. Hadn't she put this behind her?

Hadn't her confrontation with the reporter tonight proven she'd stopped hiding from them? That had been growth, damn it. So why was she reverting to a tired argument now?

Gibson's hand on her.

"They're gone now," he reminded her, tipping one shoulder against a porch post so that moonlight outlined him. "You did a stellar job turning the tables on that jerk tonight. But I wish you'd tell me if they hassled you because we should report it."

She wished he would argue with her. Debate the past. Remind her why they split in the first place. Any of it would be so much easier to bear than his concern. He wanted to take care of her, but she had to stand on her own. Because that was how she'd be again. Alone.

Added to the intimacy of the setting, alone in this house she'd once dreamed would be hers, and the way her skin still prickled where his fingers had sketched along her shoulder, Lark feared she couldn't combat the impulse to throw herself into his arms.

"I'm fine." She pressed her fingers to the center of her forehead, searching for the calm focus and grounded perspective that her patients always commented on in reviews of her practice.

Ms. Barclay has a way of slicing past the emotional noise of a problem to logically reason through the heart of it, read one of her personal favorites.

If only she had an inkling how to do that in her own life.

"Would you like to stay here tonight?"

Gibson's voice sliced past a whole wealth of her own emotional noise, stirring up all her fears for her self-preservation.

Her fingers slid away from her forehead as she met his dark gaze. Her pulse thrummed hard through her temples. Pounding. "Of course not. How can you ask me that?"

She leaned closer in spite of herself, perhaps with the need to press him for an answer.

"Because you're upset. Because there's a spare bedroom away from the media and away from the pressure of being around your family. Reporters know better than to drive onto my property. I've made that clear, and since the incident at the courthouse, I added extra security for the next few weeks until interest in my career fades." He shrugged one big shoulder. "I know being in Catamount has to come with a lot of stresses, especially now that Jessamyn and Ryder Wakefield are getting married here."

Blinking from the accuracy of every last one of his observations, Lark realized she was in way over her head tonight. From the moment she'd pulled into Gibson's driveway, she'd been giving up control of the situation. By now, her ex-husband was unraveling her every last protective layer with all the insider knowledge that a former spouse possessed.

"Now who's the therapist here?" she teased lightly,

her hands finding the tie around the end of her braid and retying the fabric. Anything to keep her fingers busy.

Away from him.

"Just calling it like I see it, since you never seem to extend the same grace to yourself that you'd give to anyone else in your life. It's okay to say enough is enough with your father. And your sister, too."

The locked box where she normally kept her emotions opened wider, the overflow too messy to stuff inside.

"Thank you," she managed finally, seeing no way to maintain an argument with him when he insisted on being kind. Letting go of the hair tie, she straightened to her full height. "It has been a rough week, but I'm committed to healing my relationship with Jessamyn. I'm even helping plan the wedding."

She caught herself before she rolled her eyes. Gibson knew how much she'd regretted losing Jessamyn to their father's side for so many years.

"Is that right?" Mischief skipped through his tone as he reached toward her forgotten braid.

Mesmerized by the careful movements of his fingers, she watched as he straightened the lopsided bow she'd left in the scrap of cotton fabric used to secure the tail.

Technically, he wasn't touching her body anywhere. Weren't the cells that made up hair supposed to be dead? Yet his efforts shifted the silky rope in a way that made her whole scalp tingle with awareness.

"Jessamyn and Ryder are in a hurry to make things official since she's pregnant," Lark rambled, needing to fill the air between them with words before the tension became too thick. Plus, the mention of any pregnancy still felt loaded for her after the way she hadn't been able to tell him about that one time when the stick had shown two distinct pink lines. Dragging in a breath, she continued, "And she's having the ceremony at Crooked Elm, so Fleur thought if we all helped, it would speed things along and give us a way to spend time together."

It really had been a sweet gesture on Fleur's part, now that she thought about it.

"I'm glad you're trying to work things out with Jess." Gibson had finished with the hair tie, but he hadn't let go of her braid. He smoothed his thumb and forefinger over the links, his gaze tracking the progress.

Sensual memories bombarded her. She had never understood his fascination with her hair, but she recalled vividly how many times he'd done this very same thing as a prelude to kissing her. Undressing her. Coiling the length of the braid around a wrist. His or hers…

Her breathing grew shallow. Her body heating with want.

When he tipped her face up to his with his free hand, she wouldn't have been surprised if he'd lowered his mouth to hers.

Instead, his voice was pure gravel when he spoke.

"Let me be your date for the wedding."

Gibson didn't know where the suggestion had originated.

He only knew that there was unfinished business

between them, and he had to find a way to see it through—had to find a way to see *her* again so they could explore it together.

Because fighting off the urge to wrap her in his arms and kiss her until they were both breathless was taking every ounce of his strength. But he knew if he gave into that hunger too soon, he could stoke the fiery resentment that lurked inside his ex-wife.

Well, sure, he could distract her with the chemistry that sizzled into a full-blown blaze when their lips touched. Yet sooner or later, she would remind him of all the reasons they didn't work. Reasons that didn't even apply anymore now that he was retiring.

Not that she believed him. And it shouldn't matter so much to him when she'd walked away at the lowest point of his career, when he'd needed her most. But the effect she had on him had never made sense.

He only knew that if he wanted a chance to be with her again, to explore the chemistry that had them both sizzling right now, he needed to bide his time. Not push for too much, too fast.

"You want to be my *date*?" Lark's eyes were wide. Her fast breaths worked the top of her fitted tank dress in a way that made his hands ache to mold to her curves.

Instead, he kept his left around her braid and his right cradling her cheek. Her skin was even softer than he remembered.

"Damned right, I do." He also wanted her to spend the night under his roof so he could make sure that she was safe, that no reporters hassled her, that her complicated family dynamics didn't steal focus from the important work she did in counseling troubled kids.

He hadn't realized until he saw her again on the courthouse steps how deeply the urge to protect her and pleasure her were both still ingrained in him. He regretted not putting her first when they were married. His mistakes were clear to him now, but how could he ever make Lark see that? He'd hurt her enough already, and he refused to do that again. Yet he needed to free himself of that hold she had on him.

Too bad the only way he could envision it happening was if he had the chance to be with her again. To indulge the chemistry until it flared out. To excise the attraction along with the hurt so they could both move on.

"That makes no sense." Her jaw tensed in his palm as she gritted her teeth.

He knew big league goalies who weren't as tough as this woman, let alone as stubborn.

"We have things to work out between us, Lark. You know it as well as I do." He skimmed lower on her braid, using the tasseled end to stroke up her bare arm like a paint brush. "Why not use your time here to end things between us the right way?"

"By dating? By attending a wedding?" She gave a half-hearted shrug of her shoulders, but he hoped she was also feeling twitchy because of his nearness.

Even in the moonlight, he could see the gooseflesh raised on her arm.

"By spending time together. We shut down everything so fast we never had a chance for closure.

To say goodbye to the good times we had instead of just the bad." He heard her swift intake of breath and stepped closer, needing to press any advantage before she shut him down.

"We might end up tearing open old wounds instead. From a counseling perspective, I don't think there's any value to revisiting a broken relationship that way."

"Then it's a good thing you're not my counselor, isn't it?" He could feel her response to his words in the rapid tattoo of pulse at her neck.

Still he waited. In life and in hockey, timing was everything.

Her gaze narrowed. "If I agree to a date, will you kiss me already?"

His heart slugged harder. Blood surged south.

"If you say yes," he teased a touch along her plump lower lip, "I'll kiss you until you ask me to stop."

Her tongue darted out to dampen the seam of her mouth. He couldn't wait to taste her.

"In that case, you can come with me to Jessamyn's wedding." She gave a small nod, sealing the deal. "You can be my date one more time."

Victory bells rang in his head, the triumph sweeter than any game seven overtime win.

"You made me a very happy man tonight." He still wrestled with the urge to run his hands all over her, but at least he had the green light for taking that sweet, sweet mouth of hers.

He closed the last of the distance between them, her curves brushing against him.

"So start making me a very happy woman." Her clear-eyed challenge was meant to provoke him to haste. Maybe to goad him into taking her hard and fast against the side of the house.

She had to know how much he wanted that.

But he wouldn't mess up this chance with her by rushing or taking more than what they'd agreed on.

"Soon enough, I promise." Slowly, he wound the end of her braid around his hand until he tugged her head back. Her lips parted as her chin tilted up.

Damn, but she was a vision with the moonlight turning her skin to cream and her lips still glistening from where she'd wet them. He pressed his thumb into the soft fullness of her lower lip, pulling it down. A fire roared inside him.

But he didn't kiss her there yet.

He brushed his lips along her ear instead. Whispering, "First, you need to let me taste you the way we're both dying for."

Six

Breathless, needy and quivering like a virgin bride after two years of abstinence, Lark couldn't wait another second.

Gliding her hands up Gibson's strong chest to hook her fingers over his shoulders, she tugged him closer so their bodies fit together. Her sigh of pleasure sounded in stereo since Gibson echoed it, his grip on her tightening as they stood alone on the shadowed porch.

Yes. Please.

She could feel exactly how much he wanted her, his body hot and hard against hers. Emboldened, she arched on her toes until their lips brushed.

Desire streaked through her like wildfire, burning away everything but the need for more. This man had always had her number when it came to pleasure, and that hadn't changed just because she'd quit using his last name. He loosened his hold on her hair, using both hands to skate down her body, thumbs barely skimming the sides of her breasts, so that she shivered into him, her nipples tightening into hard points.

By the time he cupped her hips it took all her willpower not to rock and wriggle against him, to create the friction she desperately needed. The ache between her thighs was sharp. Intense. Made all the more so by the knowledge of how easily he could satisfy the hunger.

But she couldn't let this encounter get any more out of control, could she? Instead, she pressed her thighs together in an effort to ease the throbbing. She concentrated on the way his tongue stroked along hers. Just the right amount of pressure. The perfect amount of patience. He knew her body so well, and had always taken a pride in being able to give her orgasm after orgasm. What woman walks away from that kind of sensual attention?

Already, his slow, thorough kisses were turning her inside out. His fingers had rucked up the hem of her tank dress just enough to allow his touches to trail over the tops of her bare thighs. Her feminine muscles clenched tighter, her body speeding toward the finish she needed even though they were just kissing.

Couldn't happen.

Or, rather, *shouldn't* happen. Because the logistics were all in place for her to go there. One brush of his fingers between her legs and she'd be flying apart…

"Wait." Breaking the kiss, she tried to catch her breath while Gibson studied her through half-lidded eyes.

He'd complied with her request for space instantly, a mark of gentlemanly restraint she should admire. And she did, of course. But she wouldn't have minded if he'd looked half as breathless and starved for her as she felt for him.

Gibson had always been that way though—relentlessly controlled. A lifetime of being a hockey star—from the time he was a preteen until this moment—had schooled him to be the spokesperson for every team he'd ever been on. His charm, his media savvy, his consummate composure didn't break for anyone.

A welcomed reality check.

"What made you change your mind?" he asked, releasing his hold on the hem of her dress.

Letting go of her.

The summer evening felt cooler all of the sudden. The soft chirp of crickets and katydids filled the air. Farther away, a bobcat screeched its distinctive call.

"I haven't changed my mind. I'm still going to honor the date." She didn't hate the idea really. Gibson's long absences had hurt her, but their marriage was over so she had no expectations where he was concerned.

His charm and composure might be welcome at a family wedding where she would inevitably feel out of her element. Gibson would smooth her way through the day, talking to people and keeping the focus off of her.

"That's not what I meant. You changed your mind about the kiss." He regarded her closely, like she was a puzzle to solve.

His dark eyes saw too much.

Especially when she'd let her guard down. Her whole body felt raw from that kiss. From the orgasm that she hadn't allowed to happen. Her pulse remained thready. Erratic.

"We kissed," she reminded him, backing away a step to insert some space between them. She really needed to retreat before she thought too much about how good they could make each other feel. "It was…" not nearly enough "…nice. Like always."

"Nice?" He bristled. Predictably.

Was she *trying* to goad him into a do-over? A wayward shiver tickled over her skin at the thought.

"Okay, better than nice. Obviously." She hugged her arms around herself, missing his hands on her.

Satisfaction gleamed in his eyes. "Then why stop something we were both enjoying so much?"

His voice stroked over her as surely as any touch. How could mere words set her on fire so easily?

Retreat!

"Because unfortunately, sometimes the things we like aren't good for us." She knew that from personal experience.

With him.

His head tipped to one side for a moment. Then he nodded, the speculative look fading from his expression. "Because you had a rough day with the press and your family, I'm going to accept that as an answer tonight."

"Magnanimous of you." Despite the sarcasm in her tone, she appreciated him letting her off the hook. Her defenses were in tatters and in need of serious reinforcement. Backing up another step, she bumped into the porch swing and set it rocking before she stilled the chains with one hand. "Thank you."

Gibson followed her, his moon shadow falling over her as she headed around the side porch to the front of the house.

"Just keep in mind that next time I'm going to remind you in detail how good kissing can be for both of us." He said it as confidently as if he were on camera in the locker room, trotting out an opinion on an upcoming game.

We're just going to play with the puck more and remember how effective it is to stay in our zone.

Lark shoved away the imagined sound bite in her head, telling herself she needed more sleep and less kissing to clear her mind of this man.

She arched an eyebrow. "Who says there will be a next time?"

His smile unfurled the deep dimple in one cheek that had cinched his spot on the "Men of Hockey" calendar for the last decade. "I'm already looking forward to it."

Returning to Catamount from an all-day tour of a bison ranch over the Wyoming border, Gibson slowed his truck as he neared the local diner close to supper time. Thunder rumbled in time with his stomach since he hadn't eaten all day.

He was hungry, yes. But he could have waited to grab a bite until he returned home.

The bigger draw was the place's connection to the Barclay sisters now that owner Drake Alexander had offered for his chef fiancée, Fleur, to take over operations. She hadn't done so, preferring to open a restaurant of her own down the road, or so he'd heard from the extremely forthcoming rumor mill that was the Cowboy Kitchen dining room. Still, Fleur provided baked goods daily for the operation, and Gibson had noted that one or both of her sisters frequently stopped by to give her a hand in the mornings.

Flipping on his directional as storm clouds gathered, Gibson suspected his chances were slim he could catch a glimpse of Lark now, an hour before closing time. That didn't stop him from hoping. She'd been quiet for the last few days, ever since she'd stopped by his house and flipped his world upside down with that kiss. He'd been thinking of her nonstop in the meantime and hoping she wouldn't change her mind about their date.

He hadn't intended to push her about a follow-up kiss, all but guaranteeing there would be a second. But at the time, with the memory of her body pressed tight to his, her hands stroking over him like she craved more, taking things further between them felt inevitable. Imminent.

A date with destiny.

Her silence had him second-guessing, however, and he didn't like that one bit.

His tires crunched over a pothole in the parking lot situated near the building that housed the restaurant along with a post office and hardware store, the latter a two-for-one shop. The place was as close as Catamount got to a shopping plaza, the sum total of downtown business fronts in a rural community.

Yet the parking area was more than half-full. Diner business had been booming since Fleur had taken the food offerings up a notch.

Gibson steered the truck into a space at the far end of a row and switched off the headlights while another bout of thunder rolled ominously, the sky growing dark even though the sun wouldn't set for over two hours. He saw no sign of Lark's rental car or the silver compact that belonged to Fleur, but he recognized Drake's Super Duty pickup near the entrance. Did that still leave a small chance Lark could be inside with her sister?

Trying to ignore the surge of hope as he stepped from his vehicle and settled his hat on his head, Gibson heard the bell chime over the diner entrance followed by a male voice.

"...as soon as the case is closed. You know I'm good for it." Something about the speaker's tone—the bluff confidence of someone who thought highly of himself—made Gibson glance up sharply.

He recalled that voice.

Worse? He recognized the speaker—an over-dressed out-of-towner from his too-slick suit to custom cowboy boots that had never spent a moment off of pavement. A careful comb-over and the flash of gold jewelry marked the guy as Lark's estranged father, Mateo Barclay.

Grinding teeth at the sight of the man who'd cut Lark out of his life long ago, Gibson stalled his step, still unseen near a stake body truck from a local farm. He couldn't have said what made him hesitate, perhaps an unwillingness to acknowledge the guy actively trying to steal away his daughters' inheritance.

"I'll make sure you are since your case goes nowhere without me." The man who'd exited Cowboy Kitchen with Mateo was a weathered looking rancher in worn coveralls and boots. He dropped a battered Stetson onto his gray hair. "See you in court."

A streak of lightning flashed in the sky while the two men seemed to size one another up on the step outside the diner. Gibson remembered the second guy was Antonia Barclay's tenant, Josiah Cranston. Gibson had heard from Drake that the Barclay sisters tried to evict him from the old Crooked Elm foreman's quarters, but with the estate tied up in probate, the eviction hadn't been enforceable and the guy had refused to leave.

What did Lark's slimeball father want with the disgruntled Crooked Elm tenant? Could it be as shady as it sounded?

Gibson's feet were already moving toward the entrance while the men shook hands and Cranston lumbered toward a truck towing an empty horse trailer.

"Barclay, hold on." Gibson hailed Lark's father before the snake slid away.

The man paused in the act of smoothing his pin-striped tie over a slight paunch, his comb-over lifting off his head in a sudden gust of wind.

"If it isn't my former son-in-law." An oily smile spread over his face as Lark's father walked toward him, one hand extended.

Grateful there were no reporters around to witness the encounter, Gibson disregarded the offered hand. Too bad he couldn't ignore the indignation—no, the anger—he felt on Lark's behalf.

"Paying off your witnesses already? Your case hadn't even started yet." Tension strung his shoulders tight as he stared the other man down.

Not missing a beat, Mateo shoved his hand in the pocket of his blue jacket and jingled his keys.

"I'm sure you're not referring to my business dealings with my mother's tenant," he said easily, rocking on his heels and toes. "Our association goes way back."

"I think your daughters' attorney will be interested to hear about the shared business interests." For a moment, Gibson wondered how any parent could so actively work against the kids they raised.

But then, his own father had no use for him, preferring to belittle and berate his sports endeavors, until Gibson reached the highest professional level of hockey. And while Gibson had thought he'd outgrown the need to please his absentee father, hadn't his lifelong commitment to his sport and his team been a leftover attempt to fulfill his dad's wishes? He regretted every time he'd put his team before his wife.

So yeah, he understood that it was all too common for people to use their offspring to work through their own baggage.

"Not being a man of business yourself, you might be surprised at all the ways I try to give back to the community where I was raised." Mateo gave a fake, too-jovial wave to an older couple exiting the diner as a few fat raindrops of a summer storm began to fall.

Could the guy really get away with bribing witnesses to give testimony in the court case? Maybe it would have been helpful if there had been a few reporters following Gibson around today after all. It would have been nice to have someone else's word about the shady conversation he'd overheard. Or better yet, to have to it on film.

"Generous to a fault," Gibson muttered, backing up a step since his appetite had fled.

"How about I buy you dinner and we can discuss how I can help you, too?" Mateo jerked his head toward the Cowboy Kitchen behind him. "I hear you have plans for ranching the property near Crooked Elm. I'd be glad to invest, especially since you must have known my mother intended Crooked Elm for me."

Another lightning bolt scissored across the sky as the rain accelerated. The shower pattered onto the brim of his Stetson and the tops of his shoulders while Mateo Barclay's hair molded to his head.

"You're asking me to lie under oath for the sake

of a payday?" Gibson couldn't believe his ears. The unmitigated gall of the guy. "I think my finances can do without the bribe."

A steely gleam lit Barclay's avaricious gaze as he jingled his car keys faster. "You're out of hockey now, son. It's not going to be easy maintaining the lifestyle of a sports star now that you're...not."

Gibson's fists tightened at his side. Not that he was tempted to deck the guy. He'd taken cross-checks to the kidneys from vicious blueliners and skated away without saying a thing. But if he could be this insulting to someone who'd once been married into his family, how must he have treated Lark? That ticked him off a whole lot.

Unwilling to waste words on someone like Mateo, Gibson pivoted on his heel and walked to his truck, the rain drops steaming off him as he fumed quietly. Lark had never confided many particulars about her family dynamics. She wasn't one to dwell on unhappy parts of her past. Gibson had known that her father was a liar and a cheat, and that he'd shamelessly hidden financial assets to make sure his wife and daughters didn't receive their fair share of spousal and child support. He'd played the daughters against one another, showing a different side to Jessamyn than he had to Lark and Fleur, capitalizing on a rift between Jessamyn and their mother. But hearing those spare details didn't compare with experiencing the manipulation for himself. Sliding into the driver's seat of his pickup, Gibson tossed his hat in the back and fired up the engine.

He couldn't wait another day to see Lark. Not when he needed to share the news about Cranston's testimony with her and her sisters.

Pulling out onto the county route that would take him to Crooked Elm, Gibson was still pissed off. Yet he couldn't deny that just the thought of seeing his ex-wife again, of watching her green eyes darken when he stood a little too close or hearing her fast gulp of breath when he found any reason to touch her, lifted his spirits.

He'd thought about her often, even dreamed of contacting her after his retirement, but his focus had turned to caring for his mother. And he'd come to realize that with all his doing for others, he hadn't taken the time to figure out what he really wanted.

Letting the possibilities play out in his mind, Gibson pressed the accelerator harder, more than ready to close the distance between them.

Rain battered the windows of the ranch house at Crooked Elm while Lark finished a telehealth visit with one of her older teen patients, Misty. The autistic high school sophomore had been seeing Lark for over a year, and her life seemed on track after her parents' divorce to the point that Lark had told the girl's mother they could end their sessions. But Misty herself had lobbied to extend the visits, and between that display of faith in Lark as a counselor, and the lower pressure conversations now that Misty had worked through her most difficult challenges, Lark really enjoyed the talks.

In fact, she'd purposely scheduled Misty's session for the end of the day in the hope of shoring up her personal defenses before the inevitable wedding planning.

Even now, Lark could hear her sisters charging up the staircase, laughing and juggling packages from a shopping outing to Denver. Plastic bags crinkled as they tumbled through the open door to Lark's bedroom, half falling over from the burden of dress bags, accessory boxes and paper sacks bearing designer labels.

"You won't believe all the good stuff we found," Fleur announced, dropping her armful of purchases onto the bed where an old-fashioned chenille spread and handmade quilt that dated from Lark's childhood still covered the full-size bed. "Rehearsal dress, honeymoon outfit—"

"All vintage," Jessamyn interrupted, dropping to sit on the cedar hope chest at the foot of the bed. "The store was stuffed with treasures."

Lark took in the sight of her siblings, damp from the rain but overflowing with good humor, and wondered how she could resist the lure of being part of her own family again. She'd once thought that her anger at Jessamyn's defection would last forever, but if she were counseling herself about a grievance as old as theirs, she would have to say that holding a grudge was only hurting herself.

"Very cool. Am I getting a fashion show?" She sat in the bedroom's window seat, folding her legs beneath her, content to watch them and maybe even a little grateful they'd pulled her into the fun. She'd excused herself from the outing in her ongoing attempts to avoid too much romance.

The evening planning hours with her sisters reached her personal threshold of love and marriage talk. Especially now that she'd foolishly agreed to a date with Gibson. She couldn't allow herself to get soft with her boundaries around him.

"Actually, no," Jessamyn replied, a sly look stealing over her face as she glanced at Fleur and then to Lark. "We were hoping you'd put on the fashion show for us."

"What do you mean?" Trepidation tickled her spine faster than the rain tapping the windowpane at her back.

Standing, Fleur bustled over to one of the bags while Jessamyn moved closer to Lark, finally sitting beside her on the cushioned bench of the window seat.

"I know you aren't crazy about all the wedding stuff," Jessamyn began, her dark curls growing slightly frizzy from the rain. "And that you aren't even necessarily crazy about me."

Jessamyn's eyes, the same green as her own, darted around a little. Was she nervous?

Lark couldn't remember the last time she'd witnessed Jessamyn unsure of herself. Yes, she'd seen her cry her eyes out before she'd gotten engaged to Ryder, when they'd briefly broken up. But this was different.

"I like you fine," Lark retorted, unwilling to break the accord they'd been working on for the past week in their grandmother's house. "We're working on this sibling thing, remember?"

She even slid an arm across her sister's shoulders, remembering Jessamyn was pregnant and that carrying babies surely required extra emotional reserves. The pang in her chest reminded her that she'd been pregnant once too, however briefly.

The miscarriage she'd never told Gibson about. Lark swallowed the hurt she'd thought she'd put behind her, needing to focus on this moment with her family.

"I hope so." Jessamyn blinked fast. "I know we don't have it all worked out yet, but I do appreciate you trying. And I want you to be a bigger part of my life. You know that, right?"

While she spoke, Fleur carried over a dress bag, holding it up in front of them with the black plastic protective cover still in place.

Lark glanced between the two of them before answering Jessamyn. "Um, yes?"

"I do." Jessamyn rose to her feet and dragged the dress bag up to reveal a striking navy blue gown— silk satin with a plunging neckline, skinny straps and clean lines. "That's why I hope you'll be my co–maid of honor with Fleur."

Gaze shooting from the dress to the bride, Lark tried to follow her sister's words. "You're asking me to be an attendant?"

"Yes. Just you and Fleur. I can't choose one sister to stand up there with me when I need both of you in my life."

Surprised and yes, touched, Lark met the eyes so like her own as she stood.

"I'll be there." Wrapping Jessamyn in a quick, hard hug, she realized her voice wasn't quite steady. "You didn't even need to bribe me with the dress."

Fleur squealed, joining them by tipping her head onto Lark's shoulder while wrapping one arm around Jessamyn. She was careful not to crush the gown she held. "But the dress helped, don't deny it."

Grateful for laughter after the unexpected swell of emotion, Lark stepped away from them. Outside the rain-spattered window, a swirl of headlights flashed in the driveway below. She seized on the sight as a way to reclaim a little space.

"Looks like one of your suitors is here." Nodding toward the diffused beams of light showing through the pane, Lark lifted the hanger from Fleur's hand. "While you figure out which Romeo is calling, I'll try on this gorgeous piece to see how it fits."

Fleur and Jessamyn agreed quickly enough to the plan, disappearing out of her room to greet whoever had come calling. And despite the warmth in her heart from the moment of healing her siblings had just given her, Lark couldn't deny a small twist of yearning for the happiness of their new relationships.

Voices sounded downstairs in the kitchen as she peeled off her shirt and bra to shimmy into the low-backed gown. Ignoring the thrum of a male voice too deep to distinguish through her open door, Lark told herself that tiny bit of envy was a symptom of the wedding planning. She'd hit her personal quota of romance for the day, thank you very much.

Lark had her jeans off, her hair down and the dress in place by the time Fleur's voice called up the stairs.

"Gibson is here to see you, Lark. I'm sending him up, okay?"

No!

Unfortunately, she thought the word instead of shouting it. So a moment later, she had no one to blame but herself when she stood facing her sexy-as-sin ex with nothing but a whisper of silk to shield a body suddenly very, very aware of him.

Seven

Gibson knew he had a perfectly good reason to be here, visiting the Barclay house this evening.

But for a minute, hovering at the threshold of Lark's bedroom door in the Crooked Elm main house, he couldn't recall what it might be for the life of him. Not when Lark stood in the middle of the room looking like his every fantasy brought to life. Backlit by two small sconces that bracketed an old-fashioned window seat, the woman he'd once vowed to love forever wore a navy-colored silk dress. The thin gown skimmed her curves, outlining her body in a way he hadn't been privileged to see for over two long years. Thin spaghetti straps left her shoulders exposed while the neckline dipped deeper than anything she normally wore.

Best of all? Her dark hair was loose, the way she only wore it in the evenings after her workday was done. Glossy strands framed her shoulders like a cape, catching the light as she moved to cross her arms over her chest.

A too-late effort to hide the telltale peaks of her nipples that he hadn't been able to enjoy for nearly long enough.

"I wasn't expecting you." Her voice scratched along a dry note.

"It was my turn for a surprise visit," he returned absently, using all of his willpower to draw his gaze up from her body to look her in the eye.

Then, her green gaze only took his breath away more.

"In that case, congratulations." She turned away from him to drag a small lap blanket off the window seat bench. "You've caught me completely unaware."

Her words floated around his head without penetrating his brain since the back of the gown was even more jaw-dropping than the front. The navy silk dipped so low that he could see the two dimples bracketing the base of her spine, just above the sweet curve of the world's most bite-able ass.

He swept a hand over his mouth and held it there for a second to silence the hungry sounds he made in his mind.

When she turned around to face him again she was draped in the plush white lap blanket, the corners held in one fist clutched just below her breasts. When she lifted one raven's wing dark eyebrow, an impatient expression on her face, he realized he'd better start talking fast or she'd shove him right back out the front door.

"Actually, I'm here because I ran into your father at the Cowboy Kitchen." Recalling the unhappy reason he'd driven to Crooked Elm in the first place, indignation returned. "I overheard him talking to Josiah Cranston in a way that suggested your dad would be paying Cranston off in exchange for his testimony in the case."

"Right in the middle of the diner? Where anyone in town could hear?" Her brows knitted as she seemed to weigh the news. Then she waved him into the room with a quick gesture of her hand. "Come sit. Tell me everything."

Lark dropped onto the edge of the mattress as he entered, the blue silk gown pooling around her legs as she crossed them. Even as he debated the wisdom of sitting beside her—on a bed, of all places—Gibson lowered himself to a spot near her.

"I heard them outside the restaurant, but they must have started the conversation indoors." He realized now that it had been a mistaken to drive away before going inside himself. "I was so ticked off after talking to Mateo that I didn't—"

"You spoke to him, too?" Her gaze held his, questioning.

Quickly, he recapped what happened, including her father's offer to buy his testimony and Gibson's failure to enter the Cowboy Kitchen afterward to see who might have overheard something valuable.

"It never occurred to me at the time," he explained, feeling like he'd let her and her sisters down by not thinking that through. "But maybe if I made note of the patrons inside the eatery, your attorney could have found someone else who heard your dad bribing Cranston."

Lark was already shaking her head, one long lock of hair falling in front of her shoulder. "I doubt it. My father is an expert in knowing how much he can get away with. If he was that obvious about suggesting he could bribe you, he must not be worried about blowback from potential testimony that he's unethical."

Gibson eyed the fallen lock of her hair, imagining the texture against his skin while the room seemed to shrink around them. The scent of her lavender soap teased his nose along with her mint shampoo while he remembered what it had been like to kiss her on his veranda just two days ago.

He wanted more than a taste, needed more than that. But he wouldn't rush the chance to have her in his bed and risk having her bolt. If he wanted any hope of letting this chemistry work its course, he needed to let Lark set the pace.

"He should be," he forced himself to say, dragging his gaze away from Lark to glance around the room and looking at anything that wasn't her enticing figure beside him. Unfortunately, the first thing his attention fixed on was a pile of her discarded clothes in the corner.

Crumpled jeans. Black blazer. A barely-there ivory-colored bra in a model he knew so well he could unfasten it in less than a blink. The temptation of being alone in a bedroom with her weighed heavy on him, infusing his every thought.

"I'll tell my sisters and let them decide if it's worth sharing with the attorney." Her tone was careful. Circumspect.

It was so startlingly unlike her when it came to discussions of her dad that Gibson found his gaze swiveling to her again.

"Don't you want to go after him? After the way he cut you and Fleur off from all financial support—"

"I wouldn't take his money under any circumstances," she retorted, her shoulders straightening to cover any hint of vulnerability he knew still lurked inside. "Although I definitely hate what he did to Fleur, and I resent him for hurting my mother, I'm not interested in retribution for my own sake. I won't lose any more personal happiness because of some childhood hurt."

Admiration for her pulled a smile from his lips, even as his protective instincts surged. He'd do everything in his power to ensure her father didn't succeed in his quest to steal Crooked Elm from his daughters.

He also had the power of a media following. And if he could leverage that to help Lark, he intended to use it.

"That's impressive considering—well, considering what I know of the guy," he said finally, guessing she wouldn't approve of his tactics if he told her about his plans. "Good for you, Lark."

"It didn't happen overnight, believe me." Her gaze

slid over to his as an answering smile curved her lush mouth. "Therapists know the best therapists."

All at once, the lightness faded from the moment for him as he recalled asking Lark to see a marriage counselor with him before she left for good. She'd only shaken her head and kept walking away.

Perhaps he should have welcomed the reminder of why they weren't right together for anything more than the chemistry. But the memory still nicked an old wound. And it underscored all the reasons he needed to find closure.

"Then I'll leave it up to you." He rose to his feet, doing his best to keep his eyes off the discarded pile of her clothes.

There was no point in thinking about what his ex-wife wasn't wearing under that blanket.

"Thank you for coming over." She stood with him, the movement stirring the scent of her hair again. "I appreciate you letting me know what Dad did."

"Of course." Nodding, he bit back the urge to ask her how she was holding up in the new spurt of media interest in her since that small video clip of her lobbying for more coverage of female athletes went viral. He'd tested his ability to resist touching her enough for one day. "I guess I'll see you in court then?"

"I'll be there. So will my mother, actually. She flies in tomorrow and will stay with us until Jessamyn's wedding."

He'd always liked Jennifer Barclay, but then, Lark's feisty spirit was a lot like her mother's.

"I'll look forward to saying hello," he told her honestly.

At the same time, Lark said, "I haven't forgotten about my promise to visit your mom. You'll let me know when it's a good time?"

Thinking about how often his mother asked about his "wife," Gibson knew that couldn't be soon enough. Still, he was glad Lark didn't seem to mind.

"My contractor assured me the annex on the house will be finished by the end of the week." He'd already called the moving company to bring their things permanently. "With any luck, maybe when the trial wraps up, my mom will be around."

He moved toward the door, knowing he should cross the threshold. Drive home before he looked into Lark's forest-green eyes for too long.

"Sounds good." She walked a step behind him and when he stopped to take his leave, she bumped into him lightly.

Just a brush of the blanket where it wrapped around her elbow, but the touch still jolted him.

Her gaze darkened a fraction as she looked up at him. His heart thudded harder.

Restraint, he counseled himself.

Still, he couldn't halt the final words she deserved to hear before he took his leave. "For what it's worth, that dress looks incredible on you."

She gasped softly, then glanced down at herself, parting the blanket slightly as if to recall what she'd been wearing. The renewed glimpse of her in the midnight-colored silk had him swallowing his tongue.

"Thank you. It was an unexpected gift from Jessamyn." Her fingers smoothed along one skinny strap at her shoulder. "She picked it out for me today and then asked if I would be a co–maid of honor with Fleur."

Recalling her fractured relationship with Jessamyn, he couldn't help but wonder how that went.

"She couldn't have chosen anything more perfectly suited to you," he observed, even as his hands ached to feel the fabric and Lark's warm body beneath it.

"I'm not so sure. I've never worn anything this revealing in my whole life." Wrapping her arms around herself again, she gave a small shrug.

"There are no ruffles, frills or lace. It's not a flashy color and it's perfectly tailored for you. I'd say she put a lot of thought into finding something exactly right."

"Maybe so," she acknowledged, her attention dropping from his eyes to…his mouth.

She was killing him.

One hundred percent.

And he didn't stand a chance of leaving just yet.

"Are you going to do it then? Be one of her maids of honor?" he pressed, his whole body heating.

Wanting.

Downstairs, he could hear her sisters working in the kitchen, talking and laughing. Outside, the rain still pattered lightly on the windowpane. But right here, at the threshold of Lark's bedroom, there was only the slow burn of longing.

"Yes. I'll be there for her." She dragged her focus up to his eyes. "It's a new era of sisterhood for the Barclays."

He released a long breath, trying his best to ignore the pent-up hunger. He had to walk away now before he took the kiss that she was thinking about every bit as much as him.

"Good for you." With a nod of approval, he backed up a step, inserting more space between them. "And me, too."

"For you? How do you figure?" She scrunched her nose as she stared at him, her long hair a dark ripple in the shadowed hallway as she followed him toward the stair landing.

He gripped the banister, forced himself to keep moving.

"Not only will I get to see you in that dress again, but you'll be wearing it for our date." His pulse jack-hammered at the vision that created in his mind. "At a *wedding*. Where I can ask you to dance as an excuse to have my hands all over you."

He didn't know how he'd wait to touch her until then. But at the soft, quickly stifled gasp that Lark made at his words, at least he knew he wasn't the only one who'd be fantasizing about seeing each other again.

"Lark, look this way!" the voice of a reporter outside Routt County Courthouse called to her as she strode toward the municipal building on the first day of the court challenge.

A small throng of camera operators hovered behind a few on-the-spot media members. Lark kept her feet moving, remembering Gibson's advice. Reporters couldn't hassle her or impede her. She didn't have to talk to them.

She had the control—not them.

Still, she felt glad to be entering the court with her sisters. Jessamyn and Fleur were two steps behind her. Her mother had wanted to attend the session, but a long day of travel had left Jennifer Barclay under the weather. Privately, Lark worried the stress of facing their father in a courtroom again had taken a toll of its own on their mom. They'd left her to rest in a spare room at Crooked Elm.

"Lark, are you hoping Gibson returns to Los Angeles this coming season?" A petite woman asked, taking two steps to Lark's long stride in order to keep pace with her on the left side. The awkward gait made the woman's microphone bob up and down around Lark's chin. "Is it true he's testifying here today to support you?"

On her right, a man's voice added to the noise. "Lark, have you spoken to any of the female athletes who've come out in strong support of your campaign to re-center media attention on women?"

Is that what she'd been doing? Campaigning?

It took all her effort not to snipe back that her campaign must not have been very successful since journalists like him still followed around the former wife of a major athlete rather than an *actual* athlete. But today wasn't about her battle with the superficial entertainment media types. Since her rant on camera, she'd been disciplined about blocking as many news

Get ready to relax and indulge with your FREE BOOKS and more!

**Claim up to FOUR NEW BOOKS & TWO MYSTERY GIFTS –
absolutely FREE!**

Dear Reader,

We both know life can be difficult at times. That's why it's important to treat yourself so you can relax and recharge once in a while.

And I'd like to help you do this by sending you this amazing offer of up to FOUR brand new full length FREE BOOKS that WE pay for.

This is everything I have ready to send to you right now:

Try **Harlequin® Desire** books featuring the worlds of the American elite with juicy plot twists, delicious sensuality and intriguing scandal.

Try **Harlequin Presents® Larger-Print** books featuring the glamorous lives of royals and billionaires in a world of exotic locations, where passion knows no bounds.

Or **TRY BOTH!**

All we ask in return is that you answer 4 simple questions on the attached Treat Yourself survey. You'll get **Two Free Books** and **Two Mystery Gifts** from each series you try, *altogether worth over $20*! Who could pass up a deal like that?

Sincerely,

Pam Powers

Harlequin Reader Service

sources as possible that might speculate on her relationship with Gibson in hurtful ways.

Eyes forward. No comment.

While a part of her regretted not figuring that out in time to help her marriage, another part of her knew that Gibson's extended absences were more to blame than the media. The press interference just added fuel to the fire. And how was it she ended up thinking about Gibson so often lately? She still couldn't believe they'd parted ways two nights ago without touching. She'd been on edge ever since.

Beside her, Fleur's voice pulled her from her musing at the same time as the distinctive rumble of a helicopter's rotor sounded overhead. "You okay?"

The aircraft must be flying close by, the sound growing louder still.

"Perfect," she lied, needing it to be true. "Ready to show the court what a liar our father is and secure Gran's legacy."

They were halfway up the stairs into the building when raised voices from the parking area made Lark turn to see what was happening.

At first, she couldn't quite make sense of it.

The reporters—mostly a ragtag collection of freelancers trying to invent a story to sell, although there'd been one local network affiliate—were swarming in the opposite direction of the courthouse. They moved as one toward the grassy space behind the court while the *whap-whap-whap* of the helicopter blades increased in volume.

A shadow fell over the open green area, and Lark

realized that the aircraft she'd been hearing was descending onto the lawn across the street.

It didn't look like a rescue vehicle. The gray bird touching down was unmarked. Yet why would the press think it was a big deal?

"Do you think it's Dad trying to make a showy entrance?" Fleur asked, shading her eyes as they all watched.

"Dad hates helicopters," Jessamyn murmured, craning her neck to see around a few other pedestrians who'd been on their way into the courthouse building. "I could never get him to take one in or out of Manhattan even though it's often the fastest way."

Then, the door opened and a tall man with unmistakably broad shoulders stepped from the craft.

Three-time league scoring champion Gibson Vaughn had arrived.

"What would he pull a stunt like that for?" Lark asked herself as much as her sisters. Surprised she still had air in her lungs to talk after his drool-worthy entrance.

She understood that Gibson had always been good with the media. He was often the face of the league, sought out for his opinions on big-picture issues that affected all of hockey. He'd always been able to steer negative press away from his teammates, shouldering blame for hard losses himself where he could as a longtime captain.

But for a man who was supposedly retiring, he sure was working the media now.

"You seriously don't know?" Jessamyn asked her,

spinning around to pin Lark with narrowed eyes. "Lark, he's been on a quest all week to make sure the media knows he supports your efforts to draw more attention to women's sports."

Frowning, Lark wondered why he hadn't mentioned it to her when she'd seen him at Crooked Elm two nights ago. Did he have an ulterior motive? Even as the thought formed, she felt guilty for doubting him.

"But here? Today?" She failed to see the connection between that thirty-second sound bite of her on camera with the court case today. "Why stir the press to a frenzy at the trial when we need his testimony?"

Fleur looped an arm through hers as they all watched Gibson work the crowd like a celebrity at a premiere. He walked at a normal pace, nodding and acknowledging the sidling members of the media as he moved toward the courthouse.

"Gibson has also been vocal about supporting your efforts to retain your claim to Crooked Elm," Fleur explained, withdrawing her phone and scrolling to a social media post with an image of Gibson engaged in one of his rare on-ice fights. Beneath it, the tagline read, "Hockey hero praises ex's fight for family land." Fleur flipped past it to the hundreds of comments following the post. "If you ask me, I think it's really nice he's spoken out publicly in favor of Gran's will."

Lark hadn't known any of this. But of course, she'd been so proud of herself for blocking mentions of herself and Gibson wherever possible.

"Do you think that helps our cause?" She glanced

between her sisters while Gibson drew within fifty yards of them, bringing the buzzing media circle with him. The sound of excited voices and shouted questions came with him, the volume increasing each moment.

"Absolutely," Jessamyn answered definitively, her ring-bearing hand straying to her still flat belly. "Rallying public favor makes our fight sympathetic. It sure can't hurt."

And somehow, seeing Jessamyn's fingers brush lovingly over the place where her future child rested chased every other thought from Lark's mind save one—her own baby that might have been.

She'd thought of the miscarriage all the more since returning to Catamount and seeing Gibson so often. Yet it was a hurt she couldn't have weighing on her heart through the probate trial.

"We'd better get inside ahead of the crowd," she urged her sisters. Keeping Fleur's arm looped through hers, she used it to tug Fleur toward the main doors with her. "Gibson might enjoy the media, but no matter how hard I try to flip the script, I'd still rather avoid them."

The last thing Lark wanted was more attention from the press, especially now that she knew how expertly Gibson had wound them up regarding this case. Because all it took was one reporter asking the right questions about her past—about the time of her split from Gibson—to uncover the secret she could never bear to share.

Eight

Settling into the witness stand in the Routt County Courthouse almost six hours later, Gibson's gaze went automatically to Lark seated between her sisters.

She wore a gray shirtdress cinched at the waist with a narrow belt, the knee-length hem and conservative cut of the outfit a far cry from the siren's gown she'd worn the last time they'd met. Her hair was in its signature braid, her green gaze darting around the courtroom so that she looked anywhere but at him.

Because she was frustrated with the proceedings in the first day of the hearing? Or because she was unhappy with him for leveraging his media influence to garner public support for her and her sisters?

"State your full name for the record, please," a

court official intoned while a stenographer typed away silently nearby.

Gibson had already given a deposition prior to the hearing, but today was an opportunity for the attorneys to question one another's witnesses and for the judge to ask questions about the information submitted. After sitting through hours of garbage testimony like Josiah Cranston's insistence that Lark, Fleur and Jessamyn exerted "undue influence" over Antonia Barclay in the last year of her life, Gibson was eager to set the record straight for the court.

"Gibson Vaughn," he replied into his microphone, mentally recalling the advice from Lark's lawyer to be succinct and clear in his remarks.

And he would be. He planned to nail his part of this hearing so Lark would have the portion of her grandmother's estate that was rightfully hers. He knew how much the land meant to her. He'd bought his ranch next door to Crooked Elm just to be sure they could both enjoy all the things she loved about the remote region.

Even though they weren't together anymore, he still wanted her to have what made her happy.

So after a brief swearing in and a recap of his deposition by Lark's attorney, Gibson was made available for questions from Mateo Barclay's attorney, who was allowed to remain seated at his own table. The process seemed less formal than trials dramatized for the screen, with much of the day given to dry exchanges of information for the record.

Now, the plaintiff's counsel, a tall, heavyset man

with jutting brows and a weathered face leaned closer to his own microphone to speak.

"Mr. Vaughn, your statement to this court about Antonia Barclay's personal confidences suggests you had a close relationship with the decedent in the final year of her life, but isn't it true you were divorced from her granddaughter at that time?"

Lark's eyes lifted to meet his.

And just like that, despite all the worry that he'd upset her today by stirring up the media, Gibson felt a bond with her that no divorce paper would ever erase. He could practically see her thoughts in her eyes—her silent caution to tread carefully. He hoped she could read him the same way, because he was mentally telling her he had no intention of letting her down.

"Yes, but Antonia remained my neighbor and friend."

The attorney raised one protruding brow. "Even though your divorce from her granddaughter was acrimonious?"

Heat crept up at the insinuation. His hands clenched beneath the wooden stand as he spoke evenly, "My divorce was the worst loss of my life, and I can assure you I did everything in my power to ease any pain that I may have caused my ex-wife."

Lark's right eye twitched. It was the smallest hint of a reaction, but Gibson read that one, too. Despite her disappointment in him for the failed marriage, she still cared enough to be touched by his words.

Somehow that made anything else he faced today easy.

"The photos of you with another woman online

preceding your split say otherwise," the attorney continued, approaching the bench to flash a series of papers in front of Gibson before laying them in front of the presiding judge. "As does the receipt from the moving company that loaded your then-wife's things into a truck the same weekend."

Gibson knew enough to school his features into a semblance of composure. He'd been doing as much his whole life in front of cameras, so he could perform the trick now even when the desire to lash out at the guy was strong. His divorce hadn't been about the stupid photos—taken at a charity event with a drunken attendee who'd asked for a picture with him and turned it into an opportunity to plaster herself to him. Still, he understood how the timing had looked suspect.

That charity event had prevented him from taking calls from Lark when she'd been upset about something different—something that happened hours before the drunk photos. It had been one of many times he hadn't been there for her, and he'd come to regret that bitterly. He'd been so focused on trying to lift that struggling team of young guys who'd all looked to him to turn their season around, he'd hurt the person who had mattered most.

At the time, he'd only been upset that she couldn't understand how much they needed him.

Fortunately, Lark's attorney objected to the other lawyer's remarks for all the obvious reasons, while the judge urged the man to ask a relevant question if he had one.

"Very well." Mateo Barclay's legal counsel contin-ued, returning his attention to Gibson. "Mr. Vaughn, is it true you're planning to win back your ex-wife?"

Schooled though he might be in maintaining his composure in front of a crowd, the question still rat-tled him while the attorney for the Barclay sisters ob-jected to the personal question. They'd worked out a few scenarios in case the lawyer asked about the future grazing or sale rights, but hadn't expected it to get so personal.

While lawyers and judge sorted out whether to allow it or not, all Gibson could think about was the direct query.

Memories of kissing Lark on his porch fired through him. Of the way she'd promised to visit his ailing mom.

The way she'd looked at him when he'd stood at the threshold of her bedroom, her eyes full of heat.

Was he trying to win her back?

A moment later, with the objection overruled, Mateo Barclay's lawyer circled closer to the witness stand. The older man tapped a knuckle on the wooden rail separating them as he zeroed in on Gibson.

"Mr. Vaughn, is it your intention to resume a re-lationship with Lark Barclay?"

Gibson knew where the question would lead. Him wanting Lark back in his life would give the impression that his testimony was self-serving be-cause if they ever married again, Lark's portion of the Crooked Elm property could potentially belong to him as well.

His gaze flipped to Lark's, her green eyes shooting him a warning. But since he was under oath, he had no choice but to answer with a truth he'd just come to acknowledge himself.

"Only a fool wouldn't want her back," he said into the microphone, watching every nuance of Lark's expression while her full lips tightened into a frown. "And I assure you, I'm no fool."

After the bombshell of Gibson's surprise revelation, Lark sat through the remainder of the day's hearing in a sort of fog. Dimly, she'd been aware of the aftermath in the courtroom. Her father's counsel had tried to make it sound like Gibson was a washed-up hockey player who needed his ex-wife's inheritance to make his new bison ranch venture a success now that his sports career had ended. All of Gibson's helpful testimony about Antonia assuring him she wanted Crooked Elm to go to her granddaughters certainly came into question.

Of course her father's legal team would try to undermine him, and Gibson had played right into their hands.

Since when did he want her back? The idea tied her emotions in knots. Because surely he wouldn't have lied under oath. More importantly, what did his words mean?

"Lark?" On her left, Fleur nudged her with an elbow. "Did you hear what I said?"

Dragging her thoughts from the drama of Gibson's declaration and the probate hearing, she refocused on her sister. At the same time, she realized the judge had exited the courtroom, signaling the end of the day's session. Her father was giving his lawyer a hearty slap on the shoulder while Jessamyn and Ryder were listening intently to their attorney. The few other attendees were standing to leave.

Gibson, however, still sat in the place he'd taken after he'd been excused from the stand. At the far end of her row, he scrolled through his phone.

"I'm sorry. I must have zoned out for a moment." Lark reached for her cross-body bag that had slid to one side of her on the seat, preparing to leave the courtroom. "What did you say?"

"I said you should have an exit strategy for leaving the building. When I turned my phone on, I got a million notifications about Gibson's support for us today." Fleur waggled her device for emphasis, the photo on her screen showing a split-frame image of Lark and Gibson with a dividing line between them. Words had been printed over the image reading, "Her Ex to the Rescue?"

"I'm guessing the number of interested bystanders and media hounds has tripled by now," Fleur continued. "But they're not all here for Gibson. There are memes all over the place from when you confronted the media about the lack of coverage for female athletes. That story has taken on a whole life of its own."

Tension coiled in her belly at the thought. She didn't want to be a spokesperson for a cause that wasn't really hers to champion. She'd just been sounding off. And as for Gibson's sudden declaration about their relationship, how much interest would that draw? She might have gotten a little better with handling the media, but she didn't look forward to a slew of uncomfortable questions when she walked through the band of assorted media types.

Unlike Gibson, Lark didn't have the knack for schooling her features into a neutral expression when someone asked her something upsetting. It was one thing to control her visible response to distressing news in the course of her patient appointments. It was entirely different to remain poised when someone came at her personally. Shooting to her feet, she wished she could sprint from here to Fleur's vehicle without looking back.

"Lark?" The deep rumble of Gibson's voice sounded behind her.

Sensation raced up her arms and down her spine, a strong physical reaction to his nearness that she did not want to feel. Especially when at any moment the press could be racing up to snap a photo which might capture her feelings for the world to see.

Spinning around to face him, she whispered furiously, "Haven't you done enough to upend this hearing already?"

"You're right." He laid a hand on her shoulder, a gesture meant to comfort perhaps, but it only stoked the sensations zinging through her already. "And I'm sorry if my testimony proves to be a roadblock for you."

On the other side of her, Fleur whispered in her ear that she'd be by the door if Lark needed her.

Great. There went her support system.

Her heart pounded in her chest, her emotions knotted more than ever as she faced Gibson. She didn't want this kindness from him. Didn't know what to do with it when he'd publicly admitted he still had feelings for her. Why hadn't he tried to show her that when they were married and she'd needed him desperately?

Agitated, she couldn't help but flinging back, "It's not just the testimony though, is it? What about the media interest you've purposely stirred so that no one can escape the building without being bombarded by microphones, cameras and questions?"

She looped the strap of her bag over her head, adjusting the zippered pouch to lay flat on her hip, her movements abrupt with her shaken nerves.

Gibson's hand remained on her shoulder, his broad fingers rubbing lightly as he leaned closer to speak quietly in her ear. "I know how much you hate that kind of thing. That's why I've asked one of the bailiffs about taking us out the back exit so we can reach the helicopter quickly."

She stilled. For a moment, with the cedar and sandalwood scent of his aftershave so close to her nose and the warmth of his fingers playing along her spine, she could almost pretend they were still together. There'd been a time when she would have trusted him to be by her side through anything. To be her partner.

Maybe old habits died hard because in spite of

everything that had happened between them, her instincts still leaned into that feeling.

"I don't need a ride in your helicopter," she retorted, trying to preserve a measure of distance between them. A small part of her defenses against this man's appeal. "But I would be grateful if you can show me another exit that would get me closer to Fleur's car without tripping over twenty reporters."

He hesitated, his dark eyes searching hers for a moment before his chin dipped in acknowledgment of her request.

"All right, but I hope you'll reconsider sticking with me once you see the kind of crowd that's out there." His hand slid down her back to settle at the base of her spine. He guided her toward the rear of the courtroom. "At least text your sisters to let them know we're together."

Lark wanted to argue that she wouldn't be riding home with him, and yet one look out the front windows of the courthouse to the throng of people gathered around the main entrance made her rethink that stance. Two guards had been posted by the doors to the building, a security measure that hadn't been necessary when she'd arrived that morning.

Now, with the press of dark shapes all around the oversized doors and the hum of excited voices through the glass, Lark understood how much interest in Gibson's personal life had grown exponentially in the last few days.

Stomach sinking, she withdrew her phone to text Fleur and Jessamyn. It wasn't fair to them to drag them through the media spotlight if she could avoid it by leaving with Gibson.

"Are you ready?" Gibson prompted as she sent the group message. "We need to follow Officer Kincaid."

"As ready as I'll ever be." After sliding her cell into her bag, Lark greeted the young court official dressed in a blue uniform. The man spoke into a walkie as he led them to a side staircase, taking them in the opposite direction of the way Lark had entered the building that morning.

When they reached an unmarked steel door at the base of the stairwell, Officer Kincaid spoke some kind of alert into his walkie again, then clipped the two-way onto his belt.

"Officer Bracey says your driver is waiting, Mr. Vaughn," the young man assured them, something about his straight bearing and at-ease stance suggesting a military past. "If you need to use the entrance tomorrow, just let us know in the morning and I'll meet you here."

"Thanks a lot." Gibson placed one hand on the door to push it open, keeping the other around her waist. "I'll make sure to bring a signed jersey for your nephew tomorrow. I appreciate this."

The younger man's military reserve disappeared as he grinned. "Spencer will be over the moon."

A moment later, Gibson's hold on her tightened as he ushered her from the building into the waiting black Range Rover with heavily tinted windows. Lark was too distracted by the pinpricks of awareness all through her body at Gibson's palm fastened around her hip to notice who drove the vehicle on the other side of a shaded privacy panel.

Why was his touch affecting her this way today of all days when he may have very well cost her family their case?

"Can't we just let the driver take us home?" she asked as she scooted, breathless, into the far side of the vehicle.

Away from the temptation Gibson's touch presented.

As the SUV lurched forward in the direction of the grassy expanse where the helicopter sat, Lark tried to get her bearings. A police car with its lights on sat in the middle of the court parking lot now, as if to control the extra crowd drawn by the hearing and the celebrity taking part in it.

Besides the media, there were fans from Gibson's former team there, obvious by the number of hockey jerseys and signs bearing messages to him.

"Through that crowd?" He pointed toward the mayhem now visible around one end of the building. He leaned partially over her so he could peer out the tinted window on her side of the vehicle. "I don't think that would be fair to ask of the car service since that sort of driving goes above and beyond a routine fare."

Not to mention, having to stop and inch their way through crowds of pedestrians would slow their escape and give the media hounds more time to take photos and shout questions through the windows.

Clearly, Gibson's exit strategy had been better

thought out than hers. She just resented that they had to use it in the first place. Swallowing her pride, she took shallow breaths so as not to inhale more of his distinctive scent. Having his arm braced on the window near her, his chest leaning close to hers, made her twitchy inside.

Restless. Hungry.

Was it true that he wanted to win her back? Lark shut down the question as soon as it floated to the top of her thoughts.

"If the offer is still open, I'll accept the ride home," she said instead, keeping her gaze on the gray metal aircraft whose rotors were already in motion.

"Good. It'll be safer for everyone this way. Your sisters, too." Leaning into the seat beside her, he withdrew his cell phone and thumbed a text. "I'm letting the pilot know she can take off as soon as we're on board."

A moment later, the SUV pulled to a stop near the helicopter that sat on private property behind the courthouse. She guessed it hadn't been difficult for Gibson to obtain permission to land there from the owner. Just like with Officer Kincaid, a signed jersey went a long way in getting the hockey star whatever he wanted in life.

Right now, it was tough to be upset about that because she wanted no part of facing the sports media after the eventful first day of the probate hearing. After texting her sisters once more, she took a deep breath as Gibson opened the passenger side rear door for them to exit.

"Thank you for arranging this, Gibson." The last part of the sentence was shouted, the noise of the helicopter blades drowning out all other sounds.

Taking his hand, Lark stepped from the vehicle. He didn't let go as he led her a few steps to a set of flip-down stairs leading into the chopper.

"It's my fault that all the media are on site," he returned, his own voice only slightly raised to be heard over the racket from the engine. "So it's only fair that I find a way to get us out of here."

Lark stepped into the aircraft and dropped into a sideways-facing seat while Gibson raised the stairs and pulled the door shut behind them, turning the lock mechanism for safety.

Immediately, the aircraft ascended. Gibson rocked on his heels for a moment but righted himself easily before lowering into the spot beside her. He passed her a headset and microphone before strapping one into place on his own head.

Lark fumbled with the mechanism, but a moment later, she could hear Gibson's voice through it. "Testing. Testing."

She gave him a thumb-up while he buckled his seat belt and then double-checked that hers was locked.

The small gesture of simple caring reminded her of all the ways he'd confused and stirred her emotions today. Swallowing past the lump in her throat, she spoke into her microphone as she watched the shapes on the ground move as one big shadow toward the spot where their helicopter had been.

"I can hear you," she said over a dry throat. "And I'm very ready to go home."

Gibson was quiet for so long that she wondered if he'd heard her. But then, swinging her attention back to him, she saw he watched her intently, his brow furrowed.

"What's wrong?" she asked, grateful that they were in the air and not on the ground near all those questioning eyes.

"I'm not sure going home is the best idea, Lark. The media will be waiting at the edge of the property. Particularly if they see you're there."

Spirits sinking fast, she clenched her hands into fists.

"Of course they will be," she muttered, wondering how she'd get through this week until the hearing ended. "I should warn my mother—"

Taking her phone from her bag again, Gibson stopped her with one hand covering hers.

"In a minute." A lopsided, apologetic smile lifted his lips. "Before you do that, I want you to think about how returning to Crooked Elm will only bring all of that crowd from the courthouse to your doorstep."

Anger and dismay warred in her gut. "So what do you suggest I do, Gibson? I don't have that many options."

The roar of the engine and the rotor were dulled through the headset so that Lark could hear her own breathing. Her pulse pounding in her ears with the stress of the day.

"Come with me to a private retreat in the mountains." His voice was a silky rasp in her ear, the words enticing her when they shouldn't. "We can escape all the media."

The knots in her stomach suddenly didn't feel like the result of her too-emotional day. Right now, the tension there turned sensual.

She guessed that her eyes reflected those feelings too, because Gibson's dark gaze went molten as he looked at her.

"I don't know," she half whispered the words, more unsure of what tomorrow would bring than she was about what she *wanted*.

Desire for this man still ran through her veins like he had space reserved in every blood cell.

"Just for one night, until we can make arrangements for security," he urged, his broad palm sliding over to land on her knee. His thumb grazing her thigh.

Call her weak. Call her susceptible to the Gibson Vaughn charm. But she didn't have a prayer of saying no after the day she'd had.

Licking her lips, she struggled to form words over her dry throat. At the prospect of being with him, her body tingled from head to toe, every inch of her aware of him. She knew this wasn't just about a place to lay her head for the night.

This was about *them*.

Alone. Together.

"I'll go with you," she agreed, deciding that taking pleasure for herself wasn't an act of weakness after all. She wanted him, and she owned her feelings. There was a kind of strength in that. "As long as you understand this really is just for one night."

The gleam in her ex-husband's eyes should have warned her that his notorious competitive streak had been stirred by the challenge.

But far from sending her running, the knowledge that he would do everything in his power to make tonight amazing for her only made her look out the helicopter window and wonder how fast they could land.

Nine

She'd said yes.

Gibson couldn't quite believe his luck. Even though he'd screwed up in the courtroom by drawing extra media attention to Lark's case, then added to the trouble by admitting he wanted her back, she had still agreed to spend the night with him at his retreat in the mountains.

His gaze swept over the gray shirtdress that covered her incredible curves, her shape only hinted at by the slim belt that tucked in at her waist. The silken rope of her braid had come to rest between her breasts at some point during the flight, making him fantasize about unbuttoning her dress beneath it while leaving her hair right where it lay. He would use the velvety ends of her tresses to paint lightly along her skin until she arched closer to him for more contact…

And damn, but the helicopter ride couldn't possibly pass quickly enough.

Finally, twenty minutes later, the chopper descended at a location just outside the Flat Tops Wilderness area. The pilot touched down in a clearing ringed by tall aspens, less than twenty yards from a two-story rustic log cabin.

"This is your place?" Lark asked through the headset, pointing to the structure with wide porches on the rear of both levels. Her dark brown braid shifted forward as she leaned toward the window.

With an effort, he pulled his gaze from her to glance out at the property that he hadn't visited in months. In a nearby detached garage, a truck awaited them along with a snow machine and a dirt bike, but none of that was visible from their seats in the helicopter as the rotor slowed.

Nodding, he unbuckled his seatbelt and tugged off the headset while she did the same. "It is. I bought the cabin last year, thinking I might need a place to retreat. My mother's medical team mentioned that it's important for caregivers to schedule time to unwind, and it got me thinking I might appreciate having another property nearby. I purchased the cabin in the name of a limited liability company as well so the media can't track me here."

She hesitated before answering, her expression pensive.

"You've put a lot of thought into transitioning your

mom into your house." Lark rose to her feet while he pushed open the aircraft door.

There were no houses around for miles, the view of the Flat Tops Wilderness a breathtaking sweep in front of them. And even though it was a warm day, the weather was cooler at the higher altitude.

"Maybe now you'll believe I really am retiring from hockey," he commented drily, holding out a hand to help her down.

The scent of pine rose to meet him as he stepped to the ground, the clean mountain air a welcome respite after the claustrophobic atmosphere of a small-town courtroom.

"I do. And now that I know you're committed to retiring, it helps me understand what a big change this is for you." Her hand in his felt so natural. So right.

But he let go, mindful of letting her set the pace tonight. As much as he wanted to take her inside and make her remember how good they could be together, he needed to feed her. Give her time to unwind from the hellish day she'd had in court.

"From team captain to rookie owner of a bison ranch? You'd be right about that." He signaled to the pilot once they cleared the rotors and the helicopter took off again, sending branches and saplings nearby into a frenzy of movement until it was well above the tree line. Then, not wanting to discuss the drastic U-turn his life was taking now that he'd walked away from the one thing he'd always been good at, he redirected the conversation. "Are you ready for dinner? I had a catering service deliver some options for meals tonight."

Beside him, she tensed as they walked onto the gravel driveway in front of the cabin. "Was my visit a foregone conclusion?"

How could she think that? He had championship trophies in his den that he hadn't worked half as hard to win as this time away with Lark.

"Absolutely not. I ordered the food since I planned to spend the night here either way. The construction is almost finished on the annex to the ranch house, but it's still disorganized. I've got a cleaning crew coming in later in the week to make things habitable again." Waving her ahead of him onto the wide front porch, Gibson studied her face in the early evening sunlight, hoping to gauge her reaction to the cabin. "What do you think of it?"

He stepped past her to open the security panel so he could tap in the entry code.

"It reminds me of that chalet we stayed in when we went to Vail." A sexy smile curved her lips as she ran one hand over the rough-cut log porch rail and slanted him a sideways look. "Remember?"

The shared memory lit a fire inside him again despite his efforts to be a considerate host. "Hell yes, I remember. We never did get around to skiing."

In fact, thinking about that time now—and the possibility that she might want a repeat of that incredible weekend—made him forget the security code to the cabin. His finger hovered uselessly over the panel, his attention drawn to Lark as she moved closer to where he stood.

Green eyes fixed on him like a woman who knew what she wanted.

"Lark." He'd need her help if he was going to resist her for even five more minutes. Every inch closer she came, the thinner his restraint stretched. "I'm trying my damnedest to be a gentleman—"

"Please stop," she ordered, laying her palm on his chest, right over the place where his heart pounded a demand only she could meet. She tilted her chin up to meet his eyes while she walked her fingers lower. "I'm not here for the gentleman tonight. After the day that I've had, I want the best player in the game who smokes through every defense to get to the goal."

Heat streaked through him so fast it left scorch marks. Possessiveness surged along with fiery need.

Wrapping his arms around her, he pressed her against him. Lifted her so her feet dangled off the ground.

At the feel of full body contact—even through the layers of their clothes—his breathing accelerated. He dipped his head to her neck to taste her there, the skin bared thanks to her braid.

"You taste so good," he said against her skin, his fingers flexing to cup her ass, molding her to him. "I need you so much."

Her fingers speared into his hair. Stroking. Petting. Driving him out of his head.

"I need you, too." She arched her back in a way

that tilted her breasts up, demanding his attention. "What's the code so we can get in?"

She stretched a hand toward the security screen by the door while he debated the fastest way to bare her breasts.

"Our wedding anniversary," he informed her, the answer blared into his brain now, as if all his system functions operated at her command. "Eight digits."

"You're not supposed to use dates people can guess," she chided even as she punched in the numbers.

After a series of beeps, the code cleared and the door unlocked. He never lifted his head from where he kissed his way down Lark's neck, however, he just heard the electronic cue in the back of his consciousness.

"I'll change it tomorrow," he promised, the scent of her lavender soap stronger as he nudged open the neckline of her dress to kiss the soft swell above her bra cup. "Right now, I have a goal."

Shivers raced over her.

Lark had deliberately put herself at this man's mercy and the result was every bit as tantalizing as she knew it would be. Gibson Vaughn unleashed was a power to behold. Stark male strength and raw masculine appeal made him a formidable bed partner.

Tomorrow she would contend with the complications of this night. For now, she needed one more time in his arms, one more chance to experience the way he could make her forget everything but pleasure. No one else had ever possessed that power for her, and she feared no one else ever could again.

So by the time he shoved his way inside the cabin and locked the door behind them, she was almost dizzy with lust while he strode through the foyer with her in his arms. The erection swelling against her was impossible to ignore, the heat and length of him branding into her belly. And of course, his mouth did wicked things to her breast, his tongue flicking beneath the satin of her bra cup to tease close to her nipple.

"Gibson," she panted his name as she shifted against him, needing more. Wanting everything. "Just to be clear, your goal is to be inside me, I hope?"

He lifted his head to meet her gaze, his pupils dilated so that the brown ring around them was barely visible. Around them, she grew vaguely aware of the high ceilings and open floor plan where weathered woods in gray and sandy tones dominated the space. A lamp glowed on the big plank mantel of a floor-to-ceiling stone fireplace, the golden glow the only illumination save the pink shades of sunlight from the waning day slanting through big windows.

"You thought wrong." Setting her on her feet again, he shifted his attention to the gaping neckline of her dress where he'd been kissing her moments before. Hooking a finger into the placket, he began unfastening the buttons, his work-roughened knuckle grazing first one breast and then the other. "My first goal is bringing you pleasure."

Her knees buckled as she questioned the ability

of her legs to support her through whatever he had in mind.

"That *would* bring me pleasure," she argued weakly, her words breathy and ineffectual since she swayed on her feet at his touch. Her fingers scrabbled against the expensive cotton of his dress shirt, his jacket from court long ago discarded.

Beneath her palms, she could feel the muscles of his arms working as he continued to slip her buttons free. Her nipples tightened unbearably against the satin of her bra.

He shook his head, his expression resolute. "It's been too long since I've touched you. Being inside you again is going to rip away my control, and I can't allow that until after you reach your peak at least once."

A hungry, helpless sound rose from her throat. How was it he could turn her into this needy creature at just a touch? His cedar and sandalwood scent intensified as his skin warmed. Or maybe it was the pine of the cabin walls that teased her nose with every breath.

"I want that, too," she admitted, her own fingers clumsier than his as she unfastened his belt, the smooth leather slipping in her grip. "But maybe hurry? Because I want you to feel good, too."

His eyes were molten as they fixed on hers. "I already feel better than I have for over two years."

While she tried to absorb that, Gibson walked her backward through the great room, steering her to a far corner of the cabin. Her feet stalled a little when her boots shuffled from smooth plank flooring to a throw rug, and he plucked her off her feet again, carrying her the rest of the way to a first-level bedroom suite.

More muted colors surrounded them, whitewashed grays, tans and cream. The room contained little beyond a bed and a fireplace that was bracketed by French doors on either side. He strode with purpose to the bed but didn't lay her on it. Instead, he set her on her feet and peeled off the dress he'd already unfastened, leaving her in her boots and underthings.

Another lover might have fixated on her erogenous zones, but Gibson's attention to detail had continually surprised her when they first started dating. He could spend an hour washing her hair, for example. Or endless minutes unbraiding it.

And she happened to know he liked her legs in boots. That may have been why she'd chosen today's calf-hugging pair that came over the knee. She wasn't vain about her limited looks. But a woman would have to be supremely well-adjusted to not care how she appeared around an ex.

"Were these for me?" he asked now, dropping to one knee in front of her and wrapping one strong hand around the back of her thigh so he could steady her while he unzipped the boot.

Slowly.

Oh so slowly, he lowered that zipper.

Midway down, he paused the action to stroke a finger into the skin he'd bared, from midcalf to just above her knee.

She tried to press her thighs together against the throb of need between her legs, but she only succeeded in balancing her hands on his shoulders to keep herself upright.

"Maybe. Yes." Her fingers flexed against the heavy muscles of his arms, wanting all his warmth and strength on top of her, pressing her into the bed. "Please, Gibson."

For an extended moment, she became hyperaware of his knuckle skimming up and down, up and down just inside her knee while he seemed to consider the request. But just when she thought she couldn't bear the wait another second, he shucked off one boot and made quick work of the other, tossing them aside.

In another moment, he was on his feet, tugging off his half-undone shirt and stepping out of his pants. When he wore only a pair of black cotton boxer briefs that outlined his erection, he pivoted her around so she faced the gray linen-draped bed, her back to his front.

Breathless, she leaned into him, savoring the heat of his chest. The hard ridge of his desire trapped against her ass cheek. His arms wrapped around her, one securing her just beneath her breasts, the other sliding along her belly and into her underwear.

"Do you remember my goal?" His voice had deepened. The sound vibrated against her back, tripped over her skin.

"I—I remember it." Her words stuttered as she shivered from the sensation. He stroked through her wetness, sure fingers giving her precisely what she needed, where she needed it. Not just the lush caresses that made her body weep with pleasure, but him surrounding her with his strength. His scent. His warmth.

The familiarity of it, of all the things she'd once thought she'd have forever, made a shadow dart through the pleasure for a moment. But she forced it aside, focusing instead on the circling, insistent fingers that demanded she give him everything.

"I want to feel you come." He spelled out the goal in no uncertain terms as he spoke into her ear, the words warm and damp against her skin while her body flushed with heat. "Can you let yourself go for me?"

Her head tipped against his shoulder. She couldn't have answered him if she'd wanted to since the coiling tightness inside made her breath catch. Hold.

Suspended in one perfect moment, she opened her mouth on a soundless cry before sensation slammed through her. Pleasure unspooled in one heady spasm after another, her whole body in the grip of the fiercest climax she could ever remember feeling.

Moments later, sagging with relief from it, she wanted to tell him how incredible he'd made her feel, but the throb of his body against hers reminded her that he hadn't shared in the pleasure yet.

Something she intended to correct immediately.

"It's your turn now." Spinning to face him, she gripped her braid in one hand and slid her fingers down the length of it until she reached the tie at the end.

His dark eyes latched onto the calculated move.

"Making you feel good is my turn," he told her,

stubbornly never acknowledging the heavy weight in his boxers. "You came so fast the first time, you must need another orgasm."

With each plait that she sifted free, his muscles tensed and twitched, making her feel empowered. Attractive in her own way, no matter what the world saw when they looked at her.

"I need you," she reminded him, determined to break past that competitive pride to the man beneath. Had it been a mistake to invoke the hockey hero in the first place? She'd only done it to convince him that she wanted fire and passion, not caution and restraint. "Inside. Me."

When she reached the end of the woven pieces and shook out the strands, Gibson's rough growl was music to her ears. The sound hummed through her while he unhooked her bra with one hand and shoved down her panties with the other. A moment later, he tipped her back onto the mattress, the nubbly texture of the linen spread the only fabric against her skin now.

Gibson tucked a thumb in the band of his boxers and dragged them down. Off.

She stretched toward him to pull him to her when he turned away. Confused, she followed his movements as he reached into the bedside table and withdrew a new box of condoms.

Surprise shook her. She'd forgotten about protection completely. Because of course, when they'd been married...

Emotion blindsided her.

The memories of her secret—the one time she'd been pregnant and hadn't been able to tell him before she'd lost it again—swelled in her chest. Crowding everything out. Threatening to spoil this night. This coupling that he deserved after she'd thrown all her seductive powers at the chance to savor pleasure.

Thankfully, it took him an extra moment to rip away the shrink-wrap on the unopened box, and another moment to unfold a sleeve of packets and tear one open to roll the protection into place.

Lark used that time to breathe deeply. Pull herself together. Recall the generous way he'd given to her just now.

She wouldn't allow her mistakes to steal anything else from him. Or from her either.

When his big body met hers on the bed, pressing her into the mattress with the fraction of his weight he gave to her, Lark gave herself up to sensation again. She'd enticed this incredible man, this world-renowned athlete with a body that was a finely tuned machine, into her bed.

And she would do anything in her power to make him feel amazing.

"Now, where were we?" His hips wedged between her thighs, the heat of his erection rubbing against her folds.

A whimper stole from her throat.

"You were going to make this a night neither of us would ever forget." Reaching between them, she stroked him from base to shaft, remembering how he liked to be touched. "And I was going to help."

His eyes rolled back for a moment, his nostrils flaring.

"Promise me one thing," he breathed the words on a slow exhale, moving his hips in a way that rubbed their bodies together again.

"Mmm?" She arched beneath him, ready for him.

"Remind me to feed you tonight," he told her as he entered her in one long, incredible stroke. "Because if you don't, I might forget to let you out of this bed."

A sensual thrill raced over her skin as he filled her, the possibilities of being with him this way all night enough to make her forget everything else.

"I promise." Hooking her ankles around his back, she anchored herself to him.

His pectoral muscles flexed as he kept most of his weight off her, his chest grazing hers as he set a rhythm to please them both. It felt so good. He knew her so well, understood all her cues, fed her every need.

She'd known she missed this, but that still didn't seem to account for how desperately hungry she was for his touch. His kiss.

Their eyes met again, and she wondered if this was overwhelming him, too.

Because there was no denying that what they were sharing right now felt better than ever.

"I'm going to need you more than once." He said the words with a gravity that reminded her he might consider that a personal failing.

He'd always enjoyed being able to hold back so that she could reach peak after peak.

Why hadn't she ever considered that there might be a darker side to that need? That maybe Gibson found it a challenge to be anything less than perfect?

Tightening her thighs against his hips, she cupped his handsome face in her hands.

"I'm going to need you twice as often," she vowed, only too glad to indulge them both this way. "So I hope those meals you've got in the kitchen have enough protein to fuel hourly sex."

He fell on her then, his lips tasting her deeply, tongue exploring her all over again. Then when her tongue followed his, he thrust his hips harder. Faster.

Her breath sped up as she held tight to him. Let his body carry hers over the edge with him.

This time, with him buried inside her, the sensations were different. Stronger. Better.

Plus she got to see him enjoy the finish, his gorgeous male physique shuddering with the power of his release.

Pleasure flooded through her. His and hers. Not just from what they'd shared, but from the thought of the hours they still had ahead of them to feel this way again and again. If she was only going to have Gibson back in her life for one night, she would make every second of it count.

She just hoped she could maintain her focus on the physical—the intimacy that rocked her to the core—rather than all the unresolved feelings between them. The tenderness that she felt for this man, the realization that maybe he'd found it tough to be there for her every day because he only wanted to give people his absolute best, were feelings that didn't have any place in her life anymore.

They weren't together. His decisions and problems were his own.

Yet as Gibson stroked her hair in the bedroom that had grown cool and dark now that the sun had set, Lark worried she didn't have nearly enough emotional self-discipline to keep her heart out of this night.

Ten

Balancing drinks and two warmed meals on a bamboo serving tray, Gibson padded barefoot from the kitchen into the living area of the cabin. Lark sat on a carpet in front of the fireplace, her back against the low leather sofa.

The blaze in the hearth picked out a few burnished highlights in her dark hair where it spilled over her shoulders, still damp from a shared shower. She'd wrapped herself in a gray cashmere throw blanket while he prepared their food, but he remembered only too well what she wore beneath it. Clothes from his dresser—a black pair of cotton running shorts and one of his white silk undershirts.

Nothing else.

His grip tightened on the tray at the thought, which

was amazing considering the release he'd found just half an hour earlier in the shower. And before that, in his bed. Yet already, he couldn't wait to finish their meal so he could hear her sweet cries of completion all over again.

"Here you go." He joined her on the floor, settling the tray between them. "Are you sure you're comfortable enough?"

She tucked her knees under her as she reached for one of the cut-crystal glasses of water. "Never better," she quipped, winking as she brought the drink to her lips. "I have enough feel-good endorphins floating through me right now to make me serene and relaxed most anywhere."

"Then dig in," he urged her, grateful for the way she could put him at ease even though the aftermath of this night had the potential to be awkward tomorrow. "I hope you like it."

"Are you kidding?" She lifted the lid from her stoneware plate to reveal the almond chicken and brown rice meal she'd chosen from the options of catered meals he'd given her. "I haven't been able to spoil myself like this since we…" Hesitating, her gaze slid to his. "Since we were together."

The ease he'd been feeling evaporated. He'd tried his best to provide for her when they'd split, but she'd refused every effort, insisting she wanted nothing from him.

It had hurt knowing she rejected everything he had to offer, right down to his money.

"I don't like to think about you economizing—"

"It's not a financial issue. I didn't mean that," she hurried to explain, laying a hand on his wrist, stroking softly. "It's just that I don't make time for food planning anymore, let alone order things ahead of time. And it's not as much fun cooking for one."

At his nod, she forked up a bite of her food while he tried the whitefish in lemon sauce he'd heated for himself.

"That's fair," he acknowledged, even though the lingering reminder of rejection still made it tougher to settle into the moment again. "But I've been with the same meal service for over a year, and by now they know all my favorites. I don't have to cook or plan anymore."

He was about to launch into a pitch for her to share the service with him, but before he could, Lark spoke again.

"So tell me about this bison ranch you mentioned before." She tucked into her meal again, looking at him expectantly.

The fire crackled while he thought about his answer, a spark shooting from the logs to glow briefly on the dark brick hearth before fading.

"I have a ranch manager and a business model already in place. I won't purchase livestock until next spring so I can have all the necessary facilities built." As he warmed to the subject, he explained about the animals' ranging habits, their preference to remain out of doors.

He appreciated that she was interested. Her eyes didn't glaze over the way other people's tended to when he spoke about his plans. His agent had about a ten second attention span for bison.

"You don't bring them into a barn?" she asked, brow furrowed in thought.

He'd forgotten what a good listener she was, how she engaged with him in a way that seemed effortless. No doubt, that was part of what made her successful as a counselor. In fact, long ago when she'd still been a practicing sports psychologist, Gibson had stepped into her office the first time because of a recommendation from a teammate.

But as soon they'd exchanged hellos, he knew that having her as a counselor wouldn't be enough. He hadn't continued his search for professional help, throwing himself into wooing Lark instead. But the past year he'd visited a therapist for a couple of sessions and realized some things about himself. His need for perfection in his sport. His relentless commitment to a team. Both qualities tied to his relationship with his father. The insights had helped him confirm his retirement was the right choice at this time.

Forcing his thoughts back to her question, he explained, "No barns for bison. They are tolerant of all kinds of weather conditions and get agitated if they're in an enclosed space." He told her about his trip to the Wyoming operation and his visit with the owner.

Which reminded him that she came from a long line of ranchers herself, her father notwithstanding. That made Lark's input all the more valuable since she knew a lot about the life, having spent plenty of summers at Crooked Elm.

He didn't tell her about her father's jab about Gibson's business future.

It's not going to be easy maintaining the lifestyle of a sports star now that you're...not.

The insult shouldn't have gotten under his skin to the degree it had, but the affront had lodged in his brain. He had lucrative endorsement deals that would pay out for another decade. He'd invested a big chunk of his earnings yearly. No matter what Mateo Barclay said, Gibson knew he could afford to retire and live well for the rest of his days. Yet as a real estate developer, Lark's father possessed a level of wealth well beyond Gibson's portfolio.

"Can I ask what made you choose this direction? I mean, it sounds great. I'm just surprised. When we first talked about buying property here, I thought you were more interested in a recreational ranch." She readjusted the blanket around her shoulders, the movement stirring the scent of his soap on her skin.

Stirring him.

And he welcomed the distraction from thoughts about her dad's insults.

"Well, I mentioned that your grandmother encouraged me," he reminded her, making sure Antonia received the credit for all the time she'd spent talking to him in those lonely weeks after Lark had left him. "She told me about her grandfather's horse ranch in Vallromanes, Spain, near Barcelona."

Lark's fork stilled midway to her mouth. "She did? I'm not sure I remember much about her family."

"She was trying to show me how I could build the ranching operation while I let the bison mature by exploring agritourism." He'd been intrigued by her ideas, doing online research of his own between their conversations so he could get her opinions on things as he expanded his plans. "Her granddad supported his ranch with horseback riding tours and a small bed-and-breakfast, and she thought I could grow interest in my bison if I had guided bus tours or four-wheeler expeditions. Maybe add a seasonal farmers market and pumpkin patch to draw business and build aware-ness of what I'm trying to build here."

When he realized how much he'd been speaking about himself, he took another bite of his dinner, not wanting to dominate the conversation. He didn't run that risk with many people, but with Lark he had to remember to turn discussions back on her sometimes.

"Wow. Now I'm not only impressed with you, I'm also super proud to hear how much Gran helped." She set aside her empty plate, covering the dish with the lid again and returning it to the bamboo tray on the floor between them. Then, smoothing her hands over the gray cashmere that covered her knees, she said carefully, "So obviously you're committed to staying in Catamount long term."

Something about the way she said it made him wary. He took a sip of his water before answering.

"Will that be a problem for you, having me next door to Crooked Elm? I hadn't counted on keeping the land at first since it was supposed to have been ours." Actually, thinking about that now still hurt, so he shoved aside memories of what might have been between them. "But I've grown to feel more at home here than anywhere else I've ever lived."

For a moment, he allowed himself to imagine what it could be like for them living next door to one another. They could see each other this way again and again. Indulge the connection he'd never experienced with anyone else.

"Of course it's fine," she rushed to say, her fingers moving brusquely over the blanket to brush aside invisible crumbs. "I won't be in Catamount much longer anyhow, even if we win the court case. After Jessamyn's wedding, I'll fly home to LA, so it's not like we'd be seeing each other here anyway."

There was so much upsetting in those few sentences that he didn't know where to begin addressing the problems. She had to win the case, for one thing. He wasn't going to allow Mateo Barclay to bribe his way into controlling the legacy Antonia had left to her granddaughters.

For another? He wasn't ready for her to leave Colorado. Especially not after he'd finally admitted to himself—and a Routt County courtroom—that he wanted Lark back. But what bugged him most of all was the way she seemed to whisk away any feelings she had about him living next door to her as easily as she swiped at those nonexistent crumbs.

She'd strolled out of his life once before and she seemed destined to do it once again.

Setting aside his plate, he slid the tray out of the way and took her restless hands in his, needing to reroute her thoughts. Fast.

"Just remember who you're bringing to that wedding." Threading his fingers through hers, he watched her eyelashes flutter with his touch.

Her breathing quickened.

"How could I forget I promised you a date?" She shrugged a shoulder in a way that sent the blanket sliding down her arm, revealing more of her body in his T-shirt.

Her braless body.

And his T-shirt didn't hide the tight points of her breasts pressing against the white silk fabric.

The vision proved too tempting to resist. He fell on her, his tongue swirling around the dark outline of her nipple through the material. Her back arched as she gasped, giving him more access. He sucked the peak into his mouth, greedy for the texture of her skin on his tongue.

They shifted and moved together, finding more space on the carpet so they had room to lay. Her on her back. Him levered up on one elbow to admire every inch of her in the glow of the firelight.

"I can't get enough of you." He hadn't meant to say it aloud, but the thought reverberated through him with every rapid beat of his heart.

He'd scarcely dated since their divorce, failing to find enough interest to invest in more than a night out here and there. Yet with Lark, he was all in. Aching for contact.

Needing more time.

She cupped her fingers around his neck, twining them through his hair and drawing him near as she whispered, "Try anyway."

Be careful what you wish for.

Or, maybe when it came to sensual wishes with the sexiest man imaginable, it was just as well for Lark to aim high. Because, oh my, did he deliver.

He raked off the T-shirt she wore, baring her breasts to firelight and his avid gaze. He stared for so long she knew he was strategizing a game plan for her, and she rolled her hips to urge him on. Then, his lips returned to her nipples, suckling lightly before edging back to blow a cool stream of air over one and then other. He nipped at the undersides.

All the while she worked to undress him. Finally, she peeled away the blue tee he wore from an old hockey team, revealing the compelling strength and size of his shirtless form.

"Gibson." Breathless as she said his name, the word came out in too many syllables. She wriggled her lower body closer to his and stroked the heavy ridge outlined by the sweats he'd pulled on after their shower earlier. "I need you."

He throbbed against her hand, but his concentration never broke from the attention he gave her breasts. He did move his hand over her bare belly though, his knuckles rasping over her tender skin in a way that gave her shivers. Her thighs fell open in invitation, and he cradled her core in his palm, easing the ache there with skillful fingers.

Or was he adding to the ache?

Both things seemed to happen at once, one pleasure driving the hunger for another.

How would she ever walk away from this—from him—in the morning?

Refusing to think about it, Lark reached into his sweatpants, ignoring the drawstring to find what she wanted. He'd gone commando, so there was nothing in her way as she stroked the velvet-over-steel feel of him.

"Did you bring condoms out here?" she asked, thinking the bedroom seemed a million miles away when she wanted him now.

Her heart rate galloped. She felt quivery everywhere at once.

"Left pocket," he informed her as he plunged two fingers inside her.

Making her cry out with pleasure.

Her hands forgot what they were doing as he crooked his fingers forward, finding the spot only he knew how to find deep inside her. He'd been the one to introduce her to the exquisite sensations there in the first place, and she'd never bothered seeking it out on her own. For her, solo play had always been quick and efficient. Not the hours-long extravaganza that this man could make of intimacy.

But now, it felt like a million years since she'd come this way, the pressure and tension building fast.

"Hold on to me," he entreated, one strong thigh sliding over hers to keep her still.

Wrapping her arms around him, she steadied herself, meeting his dark gaze in the firelight. Intense. Sexy.

"I'll take care of you next," she promised, wondering how he could stay so focused when she was spinning out of control already.

She bit her lip, not sure if she wanted to ward off the finish or let it roll over her.

"I know you will. But first, you're going to let me take you where you need to go." There was something about the way he said it. His absolute assurance that he knew what she craved.

Because the words sent her over the edge, her feminine muscles contracting hard and fast around his fingers where he touched her. Her whole body shuddered with it, hips lifting off the floor, spine arching.

And through it all, he worked every sweet sensation free, leaving her thoroughly pleasured and more than a little dazed. It took her long moments to come down, but when she did, she returned trembling fingers to the drawstring of his sweats, tugging it loose so she could slide off his pants.

Fishing in the left pocket, she found the foil packet and rolled it into place.

"Your turn," she reminded him, pushing him over.

He went without argument. If anything, his brown eyes flared with fresh flames as he watched her straddle him.

"I dream about this moment," he admitted, his voice rough with desire.

Or at least, she told herself it had to be desire and not emotion. Her chest throbbed an answer anyhow. Possibly because she'd dreamed about this, too.

Her throat was too dry to speak.

Instead, she gripped the length of his shaft and guided him home. His moan mingled with hers as she remained there, fully seated so she could feel him deep inside her. Then, lifting up on her knees, she stroked him up and down. Up and down.

Remembering the slow build he liked.

Remembering everything.

The rhythms that had belonged solely to them. There was nothing boring about sex that was fine tuned for maximum pleasure. Sex that fulfilled one another's every hidden need. They'd sought out all the erogenous zones. Knew how to drive each other to the precipice over and over again.

"Go as slow as you want, gorgeous," he drawled from beneath her, his eyes still fixed on her with that intense heat. "I could watch you this way forever."

He slid a hand up her hip and into the curve of her waist, his gaze tracking the movement as if she was the most fascinating woman he'd ever laid eyes on.

"Then you'd better not say things like that, or I'll get too excited." She thrust her hips twice to demonstrate.

His eyes narrowed. "You wicked, sexy girl."

But as fun as it might be to tease him, she owed him exactly what he wanted after all the ways he'd already brought her to release. Besides, she needed to make the night last as much as he did.

More.

Because while Gibson might deceive himself that they still belonged together—that he could win her back and there would be more nights like this—Lark knew better.

He'd never want her back if he knew her secret. That she'd been selfish about something she had no right to keep from him.

So she took her time giving him everything he could want from her. Every slow slide of her flesh over his. Every kiss. Every graze of her breasts over his chest.

She rolled her hips. Rocked them. Rode him.

And when her legs could take no more, she let him roll her to her back and take everything else. When he came at last, his hand buried in her hair and his other arm wrapped around her, Lark wanted to weep with the perfection of it.

Or, maybe, she needed to weep from everything they'd both lost. Everything they were losing all over again. Because as the world seemed to contract to just the hammering of their hearts against one another, one thing had become abundantly clear during the course of this night with her ex-husband.

She still loved Gibson Vaughn. And that was still a very, very bad idea.

Eleven

A phone ringing woke Gibson in the morning.

Disoriented at the full sunlight streaming through his bedroom windows onto the king-size bed, he blinked a few times to remember why he was still sleeping at this hour. Almost nine, according to a sleek black clock on one wall. But then, with the scent of Lark in the sheets wrapped around him, memories of their time together returned.

Where was she now?

R-r-r-ing!

His cellphone hadn't stopped, prompting him to retrieve it from the bedside table even as he rose to find Lark. Would she be in the shower? The need to see her, to touch her and assure himself that last night hadn't been a dream became his primary goal. His feet headed toward the en suite bath while he connected the call from—surprise, surprise—his agent.

"Dex, I'm not fielding any offers except for endorsement deals," he said preemptively as he passed through the walk-in closet to enter the bathroom. "What have you got for me?"

"Gibson, you're going to love this," his longtime professional representative began. "A contract's already drawn up and everything, with the best money we've seen to date. Plus, it's from a team guaranteed to make the playoffs this season."

The bathroom remained dark, and there were no signs that Lark had been here at all. Gibson's stomach clenched as he pivoted fast. Maybe she was in the kitchen?

"There's no such thing as a guaranteed spot in the playoffs," he said wearily, recognizing Dex's call as yet another attempt to woo him back into the game. "And it doesn't matter anyway because I'm not playing anymore."

He paused in the bedroom to throw on his T-shirt and sweats from the night before, noting that Lark's clothes were gone. Which only meant she'd already dressed for the day, right? Glancing out the bedroom window at the Flat Tops Wilderness all around the cabin, he reminded himself she couldn't have gone far. They'd taken a helicopter in, for crying out loud. It wasn't like she could walk to Crooked Elm from here.

Why hadn't she curled up next to him and awakened him with a kiss, the way she had when they'd been married?

"Gibson, you're the biggest story in sports media this week. I couldn't have scripted a better way for you to command a new contract—"

"And that's part of the problem," he shot back, unable to scavenge even an ounce of the composure he'd been famous for on camera throughout his career. Had his agent's machinations behind the scenes helped ratchet up interest in Gibson's career transition? Was Dex planting seeds around the media to drive coverage of an angle that wasn't ever going to happen? "My life is more than a sound bite, and I'm not a clickbait story anymore."

Striding into the kitchen with fast, angry steps, he knew at a glance Lark wasn't there. A piece of paper lay on the butcher-block countertop that hadn't been there the night before.

A note?

Knowing it wouldn't contain anything good, he approached it slowly, still hoping she'd walk through his front door. Say she'd been out for a morning walk and couldn't wait to shower together.

"But, Gibson, as your agent it's my job to share all offers with you—"

"Not anymore it isn't." Gaze fixed on the torn scrap of notebook paper held in place by a black pepper grinder, he wouldn't let himself look at it until he'd dealt with the call. "If you want to keep repping me for the occasional speaking appearance or ad deal that may come through in the future, you're going to have to spread the word with the media that I'm out of hockey for good. Do we understand one another?"

He regretted not taking a more aggressive stand on the issue earlier in the summer when it might have kept Lark from being hassled. But he was done being the face of any franchise. Done being the last guy to leave the locker room so the media had all the quotes they needed to file their stories. Done sacrificing everything—including his personal life—for the sake of the game.

"Loud and clear," Dexter said finally, his tone thoughtful. "I'll share your intentions on my end. But keep in mind it hasn't been me working the media all week to garner public support for your ex-wife's court case."

The comment found its mark.

"True enough. That's on me." He'd used the media when he thought it might help Lark, but now that he knew how vehemently she opposed those tactics, he wouldn't be tempted to leverage that tool again. "I've got to go now, Dex. I'm expecting a visit from you next spring when I've got my bison on the property. We'll catch up."

He tried to end on a positive note, not wanting to burn bridges to make his point. Losing Lark once had made him realize he needed to work harder to be a better man.

"For you, I might take a whole day off," his agent mused before they disconnected.

Gibson might have felt relieved to have gotten his message across since it meant he'd at last made peace with retiring. He had a new career to look forward to, and whether it was a financial success straight out of the gate didn't matter. Or rather, he couldn't allow it to matter. He needed a path in life that wasn't predicated on society's metrics for success.

He intended to find something that would bring him some happiness and a sense of purpose so he could rewire all the negative habits of his brain to associate success with the stat sheets. From now on, he wasn't going to be tracking goals and assists or number of all-star appearances.

Too bad he'd learned how to do those things just in time for Lark to leave him nothing but a note on his kitchen counter.

Sliding the paper out from under the pepper grinder, he unfolded it and read,

I asked Fleur and Drake to pick me up on the way to court this morning. I'm behind on my share of maid of honor duties, so I'll be busy this week, but I won't forget our date.

No mention of their night together. No hearts or smiles to indicate any warmth of feeling for what they'd shared. And yes, call him ten kinds of sucker for caring that she hadn't drawn any damn smiles in the margins.

He cursed softly, swiping a hand over his unshaven jaw. The kitchen felt too big and impersonal with only him standing in it, like all the warmth of the day had faded when Lark walked out of his house.

Again.

She wanted space from him, obviously. He'd given

it to her the first time she'd run off when they'd been
married, and he'd regretted it. Now? He wasn't sure
he could let her go again.

Gritting his teeth, he stalked toward the bathroom
to shower. He had a court trial to attend.

From her seat between her sisters in the second
row of the Routt County courtroom, Lark had a clear
view of Jessamyn's fiancé, Ryder Wakefield, as he
shared his testimony for the record.

She discreetly checked her smart watch for messages while Ryder related some background on himself. Still no word from Gibson. Not that she expected
any given the cowardly way she'd left his cabin early
that morning. By dawn, with her body thoroughly
sated, her heart tender and hopeful, she'd known she
didn't have the emotional reserves to paste on an
"everything's fine" morning-after smile. So she'd
called Fleur and crossed her fingers Drake would
know the location of Gibson's cabin to retrieve her.

And while Lark had been relieved to slip out un-
heard, she still felt like a first-class heel for not being
able to face Gibson after all they'd shared. Even now
her body ached pleasantly from his attentions. Too
bad the twinges in her chest were far from pleasant.

Straining to ignore the feelings, Lark looked to
Ryder on the stand. His story was compelling, even
as it revealed the very worst of her father's character.
She'd heard secondhand about Ryder's presence in a
search and rescue mission on a mountain peak after
Mateo Barclay's then-girlfriend had been critically

injured. But the tale was even more upsetting to hear from Ryder's point of view now.

Mateo had been frustrated with the girlfriend who couldn't hold her own on skis and had explained to Ryder that he "preferred strong women who could keep up." That alone made Lark feel ill—not only because that was the mindset of the man who'd raised her, but also because of all she'd learned as a counselor about the way a parent's biased gender views could undermine a child's sense of self. Yet, Ryder wasn't done.

While the Barclay sisters held their collective breath for the rest of the testimony, Jessamyn reached to hold Lark's hand. Surprised, she glanced to her left to see a tear slide down her sibling's cheek, a reminder that Jessamyn had striven to be the "strong woman" in their father's eyes for nearly a decade after Fleur and Lark had quit trying to please him. For the first time, she saw Jessamyn's journey through a therapist's eyes instead of a sister's. Lark knew all too well the way an adult child could continue seeking approval without being aware of how damaging it could be when that approval would never be given. She guessed that same sort of need for approval had driven Gibson for most of his career too, not that he'd ever said as much.

As for Jessamyn, had the pricey education and career opportunities she had received ever made up for the love she hadn't gotten?

Squeezing Jessamyn's hands in hers, Lark reached

to take Fleur's palm in her other. Braced together, they listened as Ryder continued.

On the stand, Ryder cleared his throat, his eyes seeking his fiancée's before he went on. "Mateo said that's why he left his wife when Jennifer Barclay began to struggle with depression. He viewed that as weak."

Lark felt a fierce stab of relief that her mother hadn't attended the trial, even as Mateo's lawyer interrupted Ryder to remind the court that his client had likely been suffering from shock that day. The attorney had already tried twice to have the statement suppressed on the grounds that Ryder had been serving in an EMS capacity that day, and that Mateo's remarks were subject to doctor-patient confidentiality. The judge, thankfully, had not agreed.

While the legal representatives argued, Lark heard a murmur in the back of the courtroom. Turning, she caught sight of Gibson slipping into a seat at the rear of the room.

"Gibson's here," Fleur observed quietly in her ear.

As if Lark didn't have every sense attuned to the man at all times.

He'd come to the trial even though he hadn't been scheduled to testify today? Her heart fluttered at the proof of his caring. The support warmed her in spite of the swirl of tangled emotions at the sight of him—guilt for leaving, hunger for his touch, regret that she might never feel his kiss again.

He wore a gray suit today, his white dress shirt unbuttoned at the throat while he made himself comfortable at the end of a bench. A moment later, his dark gaze met hers, as if he'd felt her watching him.

What did he discover written in her face, she wondered? She didn't know how she felt about seeing him, so she couldn't imagine he could glean any more understanding about her feelings than she had herself. Her belly tensed with nerves.

As the lawyers finished their debate, Lark returned her focus to Ryder on the stand. After prompting from the judge, Ryder continued to speak.

"Mateo Barclay went on to tell me that his mother had disinherited him because of how he'd treated his ex-wife," Ryder explained, giving what Lark considered to be the most important piece of evidence in the defense.

Because Ryder's testimony proved that Mateo knew nine years ago that he wasn't receiving an inheritance from his mother.

More questions followed from Mateo's lawyer, but Lark didn't pay much heed to the back and forth. The key statements had been made for their case, so now they needed to trust the process. That the court would find Gran's will valid and Crooked Elm would rightfully belong to Lark, Jessamyn and Fleur.

If the judge decided in their favor, they'd be able to kick Josiah Cranston off the land for good, and they could send their father packing.

And whether or not the judge decided in their favor, Lark had done all she could here.

Once the decision was in she'd be free to leave Catamount—and Gibson—right after Jessamyn's wedding. Lark would be able to say she'd made progress toward healing her relationships with her sisters, and she'd done what her grandmother would have wanted by spending time here with them for the summer.

There was nothing left to keep her here. Right?

Surely, that knowledge should bolster her as she started the next chapter of her life alone in Los Angeles once again. Or maybe it would if she could look herself in the mirror and feel like she'd been honest with Gibson, too.

She really did owe him the truth she hadn't been able to share during their marriage. He would be angry. Rightfully so. But that didn't excuse her from something she should have confided to him long ago. Maybe then, she'd be able to leave town with a clear conscience.

Too bad she'd also be leaving with a heart more tattered than ever. Without thinking, she squeezed Jessamyn's hand again. Taking comfort for herself when she should have been giving it.

"How are you doing?" Lark whispered to her to cover the action.

At the same moment, the judge announced a short recess for lunch, then rose to leave. The participants in the case began conversations of their own, gathering bags and keys in preparation for the break.

Jessamyn nodded quickly, sliding her hand free from Lark's. "I'm okay, thanks. I just hope Ryder's testimony is enough to prove that Dad knew Gran's wishes long ago."

"Me, too." Standing, Lark's gaze went to where

Gibson had been sitting, but there was no sign of him now. "But we've worked hard to find as many people as possible who knew what Gran wanted. Now we need to let the legal process play out."

Even as they moved toward the exit, Lark's eyes scanned the room for Gibson. She should be relieved, perhaps, since she'd been the one to flee his house the morning after their amazing night together, telling him she'd see him on their date for Jessamyn's wedding. Implying, of course, that she wouldn't be seeing him before then.

Yet she couldn't deny the twinge of disappointment at his absence.

He'd come to support her family, perhaps. But now she realized it hadn't been to see her.

Cursing herself for being sad about getting exactly what she'd told him she wanted, Lark stuffed down the pain her chest and told herself to get over it.

Especially as Fleur and Drake paired up in the corridor outside the courtroom. And then Ryder and Jessamyn did the same.

Leaving Lark very much alone.

Gibson stared at the desk calendar in his home office, mentally checking off how many days he'd managed to stay away from Lark since she'd vanished from his cabin.

Five.

Five endless days of scarcely seeing her face except for their brief acknowledgments of one another at the courthouse, surrounded by other people. He'd continued to attend the sessions in case he was needed to clarify a point of his testimony and also to show public support for the Barclay sisters. At least the media interest had died down after Dex had issued a statement to the press that Gibson was committed to retiring, but a few stubborn freelancers still stuck around Catamount, hoping for a story.

The coverage of the estate case had slowed down too, and that was just as well since Lark hadn't been pleased at Gibson's efforts to involve the media. Yet another way she hadn't wanted what he'd had to offer. Still, he could see her point since the intrusiveness of the cameras and questions bothered him more than it used to. He understood why it had upset her so much during their marriage.

He just hoped the judge in their case reached a decision soon. And he hoped like hell Lark and her sisters would receive the lands Antonia had intended for them.

"Gibson, are you in here?" His mother's voice called to him from the annex on the far side of his kitchen.

She and her caregiver had moved in with him the day before since the renovations on the house were complete. The transition had seemed to go well enough, even though his mom had told him several times that she really needed to get home soon.

"I'm on my way, Mom." Dropping his pen onto his desk, Gibson strode out of the office and into the kitchen where his mother stood at the door, peering out through a side light. Her blond hair was pinned back from her face, her frosted pink lipstick the same shade he remembered from childhood. She didn't even look her age, let alone old enough to be suffering from dementia. He swallowed a swell of emotion before he asked, "Is everything okay?"

"Someone's in the driveway, Joe. Come see." His mother called him by his father's name, a slip she'd never made before.

Was she getting worse? What other signs might he have missed?

"It's Gibson," he reminded her gently, draping an arm over her shoulders to hug her to his side before he glanced out the leaded glass windowpane. Outside, the tall, familiar figure of his ex-wife made her way up the walk, her dark braid bouncing with her step.

Lark was here.

The emotions that knowledge stirred were too dense and multilayered to name. But first and foremost, he was grateful as hell that she was going to be able to visit with his mom before the illness stole even more of her.

"Who is it?" his mother asked, peering up at him with confusion in her eyes.

A pang filled his chest. He hated the unfairness of this disease with every fiber of his being.

"That's Lark, Mom," he explained, rubbing an encouraging hand on her shoulder. "You've been wanting to see her."

Recognition flooded her expression along with genuine joy.

"Lark's here." His mother smiled, every trace

of confusion fading as she swatted his chest good-naturedly. "Of course I want to see her, you silly man. Open the door!"

Before Lark could lift her hand to knock, Gibson did as his mother asked, swinging the door wide, bracing himself for the impact of her presence.

He only had a moment to make eye contact with her before her gaze darted to his mother at his side. And then Stephanie Vaughn stepped forward to fold Lark in her arms.

"Hello, my favorite daughter-in-law." His mother squeezed her tight while, over her shoulder, Lark shot him a questioning glance. "It's so good to see you."

It was too late for Gibson to give Lark any warning or explain how much his mom's condition had progressed, but Lark was a mental health professional. She would surely assess the situation quickly enough for herself.

Even though it might be awkward.

Really awkward, actually, considering his mom thought they were still married.

Twelve

Lark's reasons for coming to see Gibson all moved to the back burner when she stepped into her former mother-in-law's warm embrace.

She'd come to tell him the judge had ruled in their favor. To announce that their father's claim had been denied. And to celebrate that Crooked Elm and all of Antonia Barclay's estate would be legally distributed between Jessamyn, Fleur and Lark. Their father had already left town, swearing never to return. She'd wanted to thank Gibson for his testimony and support, but her joy in a victory over her father had been overshadowed by her need to tell Gibson about the secret she'd been carrying. The one she feared would sever their connection for good.

Now? With Stephanie Vaughn looping her arm

through Lark's and leading her into the new addition Gibson had built for her, how could she do anything but settle in for a visit?

"This is really beautiful," Lark remarked sincerely, glancing around at the wide windows overlooking the pool house and backyard, the separate entrance from the driveway in front, and the two first-floor bedrooms to accommodate Gibson's mother plus the caregiver that he'd mentioned.

The small kitchen had a Scandinavian appeal with its clean, modern lines and spare, blue and white touches, the open floor plan connecting the living area with dark blue couches and lots of greenery.

"Thanks to you and Gibson," Stephanie told her, waving Lark toward one of the couches. "Let's sit."

Confused, Lark lowered herself onto the seat she'd indicated. "Oh, but it's Gibson who—"

"Lark, can I get you anything to drink?" Gibson interrupted her, something she'd never known him to do.

But then, his whole manner seemed anxious. He hovered close to them, staring hard at her. Meaningfully. Like he wanted to communicate with his eyes.

She had no idea what he was trying to tell her though.

"No, thank you. I'm fine." Scooting deeper into the corner of the sofa, she glanced toward his mother, thinking she looked the picture of good health. Not that her appearance necessarily meant she was thriving. Lark understood better than most how mental health challenges could hide behind deceptive facades. "Are you all settled into the house now, Stephanie?"

Tall and lean, Gibson's mother tucked her ankles to one side as she leaned forward to visit, her spine arrow straight. She'd always had that noble bearing about her, making Lark want to improve her own posture. Yet there was nothing else remotely intimidating about her. She was warm and chatty, the kind of person content to carry on a one-sided conversation if her companion felt quiet, and that worked for Lark just fine.

Given how her job necessitated drawing people out conversationally, it had often felt like a relief with her former mother-in-law to just listen. And it had been ages since they'd spent time together. Gibson had been away so much during the last six months of their marriage that Lark had few opportunities to see his mom.

"I am all situated, thank you." Stephanie smoothed a manicured hand over a blue throw pillow. "Gibson moved my furniture so I'd feel at home," she mused as she stroked the soft pile of the fabric. Then, she lifted her gaze to look at Lark. "But it won't really feel like home until we all sit down for a meal together."

Surprised at the invitation, Lark hesitated. Things were uncomfortable enough for her since she needed to speak to Gibson privately and tell him about the secret she'd kept from him. But to suspend that task in order to sit through a tense meal with him?

Before she could answer, Stephanie hastened to add, "But it's your house, dear. I don't mean to invite myself over before you're ready. I just think it will be nice for us all to catch up as a family." Reaching across the couch cushion to Lark's side of the sofa, she squeezed her hand. "Gibson, you should bring your wife that water after all. She looks a little pale."

Realization swept over her. Hard.

Stephanie thought they were still married.

Lark's gaze shot to Gibson's face. She read the apology in his eyes this time. His helplessness in the face of his mother's merciless illness.

When had Stephanie gotten so much worse? She was only in her early sixties.

"I will get her some, Mom," Gibson assured her, coming to Lark's rescue. "Why don't you show her where we set up the doll collection?"

Stephanie's blue eyes brightened as she nodded. "Of course." Rising from the couch, she gestured for Lark to follow her toward the bedroom. "I'm preserving the dolls for my granddaughter one day. I hope it won't be much longer, you two!"

Lark's step faltered, the lighthearted remark smacking her like a two-by-four to her midsection. Her hand went to her mouth to stifle a gasp.

How much crueler could this day get?

Pretending she was married for the sake of Gibson's mom. Smiling through prompts to make a baby with the man she'd once loved and now loved all over again without him knowing. All while carrying this awful secret that weighed on her like lead shoes.

It hurt that Gibson hadn't bothered to tell her about his mom's deterioration when he'd invited Lark to visit. He must have known even then how tough it would be for Lark to smile through the pretense that they were still a couple.

Or what if she'd unwittingly revealed the divorce to Stephanie?

Still, she had zero right to be indignant about his secrets considering her own, but that didn't stop her from feeling frustrated. Hurt. And battling the urge to flee.

"You okay?" Gibson's voice sounded low beside her as he caught up to her in the corridor. He passed her a glass of water, his fingers brushing hers while his mother led them into one of the bedrooms.

"Not even close," Lark fired at him, edgy and overwhelmed. "We need to talk."

"And we will. She tires more quickly these days, and her caregiver will return in an hour." The sadness in his voice at the mention of his mom's health reminded her how much he'd been dealing with on his own. "We'll speak then."

Heart softening, she nodded. "Fair enough."

Until then, she would visit with her former mother-in-law and look at the dolls for the baby Lark wasn't meant to have.

He should have warned her about his mom.

Gibson had recognized it the second Lark's panicked eyes had sought his when his mother referred to her as his wife. He'd had years to watch the slide of his mom's mental health, but the last time Lark had seen her, she'd been merely forgetful.

Not overtly confused and disoriented.

Now, as his mother's caregiver ushered him and Lark from the annex he'd built for them, Gibson prepared himself for whatever Lark wanted to discuss with him. Sure, he recognized that she was probably frustrated that he hadn't prepared her for this visit. But she'd made the trip to his place even before she knew his mom would be there, so clearly there was more on Lark's mind than just what had happened today.

He knew better than to hope that she wanted a repeat of their night together. Her silence for days on end had assured him she viewed that as a one-time event. And yes, that still stung.

"Do you have any tea?" Lark asked him now as they moved into his kitchen.

Her voice sounded weary. And of course, tea was her comfort drink, so he knew she felt stressed.

"Chamomile or orange spice?" he flipped the switch on the countertop kettle before pulling two mugs from an overhead cabinet.

"Chamomile. Although I'm not sure there are enough calming vibes in those tea leaves to soothe the frustration I'm feeling that you didn't tell me your mother thinks we're *still married*." She dropped into one of the seats at the kitchen island, her head slumping forward to rest in her hands.

Regret pinched. He cleared his throat to explain, but her head popped up, her eyes blazing.

"Gibson, how could you not mention her condition to me? When I asked her caregiver how long she'd been with your mother, she said over two years. Which means you hired her while were still together." Her volume rose at the same time the kettle beeped for the water. "Regardless of what happened between us, I care about your mom."

Grateful for the extra moment to formulate a reply, he took his time pouring two cups of tea.

"I hired her during a stressful time for us. The media coverage had really intensified for you and we were dealing with our own problems. I didn't want to add to that." Lifting the mugs, he pivoted to the island, sliding one in front of Lark and keeping the other one for himself.

"But she's family. At the time, she was my family, too."

He rubbed his nape. "I know that, Lark, but I worried you might feel an undue burden to help because you're a mental health professional, and that wouldn't be fair to you." He slid into the seat next to her at the island.

"I would have wanted to help, but you robbed me of the chance." She pushed aside the cup he'd poured and swiveled on her barstool to face him fully. "You carried everything in your world on your shoulders, never sharing with me. So is it any wonder I felt like I had to do the same?"

"You felt like you had to shoulder your burdens on your own," he repeated, recognizing that she was upset and not quite following why she was *this* upset. He'd been trying to protect her, damn it. Why was that so wrong?

Sure, he understood that she had wanted to be a bigger part of his life and he'd denied her that by trying to manage his problems alone. In retrospect, that hadn't been fair to either of them.

But he felt like he was missing something more.

"That's right," she snapped, sliding off the stool to pace the length of the kitchen, agitated energy fairly vibrating off of her as she moved. "In case you missed it, I pride myself on being independent, too. That's why I never asked to travel with you, because I knew you liked the time on the road to bond with your teammates."

Surely he hadn't heard her correctly.

"Wait. You would have come on the road with me?" He wanted to slow down and talk about that, because he would have appreciated her steadying presence in that last crap year when he'd been with the LA team and the media had lambasted his team and him at every turn.

"So no matter how hard it was to stay at home and live like a single woman while my husband kept an existence separate from me, I did it because I knew what I had to deal with was nothing compared to the pressure the team and the media put on you." She reached the window and swung around to pace the length of the room again, her arms crossed tight around her body. "And you, Mr. Calm and Composed, Face of the Franchise, never complained that you had too much on your plate."

Gibson was out of his depth. But then, he'd never

JOANNE ROCK   185

seen Lark this upset. Except, of course, for the night
she'd walked out on him.

Rising to his feet, he moved closer to her without
interrupting her path. He wished he had the right to
wrap his arms around her and slow her down. To hold
her tight and tell her everything would be all right.
"Lark, please. What's going on here? Is this all about
me downplaying Mom's problems? Because I know
I should have told you—"

"No. It's not about that." Stopping her restless
prowling, she pinched the bridge of her nose. "Although I'm hurt about that, I didn't come here to argue
with you about what happened in the past."

Her tone shifted. Growing cooler. Calmer. And
yet, the change made him wary. She stared at him
with steady green eyes, as if steeling herself.

"Okay." He reached for her, wanting to take her
hand in his, but she sidestepped him to move back to
the counter stool. "What did you want to talk about
then?"

He rested his elbows on the gray-and-white quartz
but remained standing. His eyes followed Lark's
movements as she sipped her steaming tea. The scent
of chamomile filled the air.

She continued, "We had a chance to chat after the
judge gave his decision. Jessamyn and Fleur plan to
stay in Catamount. Fleur can go ahead with her ideas
for a restaurant on the land. And we'll give Josiah
Cranston thirty days to vacate the premises."

He'd be glad to see the last of the ranch's shady tenant who'd been willing to lie under oath for a payday.

Gibson reached across her for his own mug of tea, wishing they could return to the night they'd spent at the cabin. When every conversation hadn't been fraught with land mines, and they'd been deliriously happy just to touch each other. Take care of each other.

"There will be a celebration at the Cowboy Kitchen for sure," he mused as he took a sip of the drink. "Fleur is the most talented chef this sleepy town has ever seen."

For an instant, he thought he spied an answering light in Lark's eyes. But it faded again, and she drew a long breath.

"I also came by to let you know that I'm leaving right after Jessamyn's wedding this weekend." When he made to interrupt, she held up a finger to indicate she needed another moment. "And it only seemed fair that I let you back out of our date ahead of time. I think you'll want to when you hear something that I should have shared with you a long time ago."

Warning prickled the skin at the back of his neck. Wariness tightened his muscles. The feeling was reminiscent of the foreboding he'd had the day he'd pulled up to their house, only to discover she was leaving. But this couldn't be the same because they weren't together now.

"We agreed to attend the wedding together. I'm looking forward to it." He knew there was nothing she could tell him that would change his mind about wanting to work things out between them.

But had he urged things forward too fast with his

public declaration under oath? Was this her way of pushing back?

"Please listen, Gibson. This isn't easy for me." Her gaze fell on the double-sized refrigerator. The open shelving near the sink. Shifted down to her tea mug. Anywhere but on him. "I never told you why I was so upset that night of the charity event when you were on the road and couldn't take my calls."

He mentally rewound to the time she referenced. The evening of the photos of him with an intoxicated patron of the event, photos that showed the woman stuck to him like a second skin and him wearing an awkward smile since he hadn't known how to peel her off.

Had that played a larger role in their split than he'd realized? Lark had never seemed ruffled by incidents like that before.

"Those pictures were misleading, like I explained in court." He'd always tried to make himself accessible to fans when he'd been playing, knowing they made his lifestyle possible. For the most part, he didn't regret it since the vast majority of fans were incredibly supportive.

But he fiercely regretted that evening when a woman had taken advantage of their proximity.

"I know that." She met his eyes finally, her expression sincere. Compassionate. "I've seen with my own eyes how some fans cross boundaries." A sad smile lifted one corner of her lips. "As a woman, I understand a thing or two about being the object of inappropriate touching, believe me."

A surge of protectiveness roared to life inside him, and he was seized with the need to right the whole world for her. But he knew better than to trail down a tangential path when she wanted to share something important with him.

"Then what about that night?" he asked gently, hating that he hadn't tried harder to find out before now. But he'd been so caught up in his own problems with his mother and his team, compounded by the pain of Lark leaving him, that he hadn't had the emotional wherewithal to seek out the "whys." Or at least, not as tenaciously as he could have. "What happened?"

"I miscarried."

The two words rattled through him on a discordant note, making no sense.

"You…" He struggled to remember that night. The long weeks apart that had preceded it when he'd been on a road trip, exacerbated by a home stand with one charity event after another as part of the team's PR during a year of poor performance in the rink. He and Lark had hardly seen each other. But still, she hadn't said anything to him about… "You were pregnant?"

He didn't even dare think about what that meant. Had she been happy about it? Unhappy, given how disconnected they'd grown in those last few months together? The idea that his child might have been unwelcome news was a sucker punch he would have never predicted. Still, he tried not to let his thoughts run away with him until she finished explaining.

She swallowed hard, her eyes downcast. Slowly, she nodded.

"Yes. I was only ten weeks along, but—"

"Ten weeks?" He did a double take, brain casting back even further in the past to remember the circumstances in their lives during that time. "How long did you know about it?"

She exhaled a long breath, as if trying to calm herself. He needed some serious calming too because the news was pummeling him.

"About three weeks. It took me a while to realize I was late, and even then I thought it was just stress because of everything we were dealing with. The increased media scrutiny, the insinuations about our marriage, your travel schedule—" She stopped herself. Shook her head. Arms wrapped around her stomach. "Anyway, by the time I took a pregnancy test and saw a doctor, I was already over six weeks. And I knew the exact window of conception since you weren't home very often."

Regrets about that and so much more carved a hole in his chest.

"I knew we'd grown apart, but for you to not even tell me you were pregnant…" He let the words trail as he traced the rim of his mug with his thumb, the scent of chamomile not nearly enough to soothe the raw parts inside him.

"I tried at first. I swear I did." She laid a hand on his knee, her touch urgent. Squeezing. "I made a dinner for us, with a cake that had the pink lines on it, just like the pregnancy test."

He was afraid to ask where he'd been for that dinner that hadn't happened. "I know I wasn't around much—"

"You decided to do a training camp for kids with your friend in Nova Scotia that weekend instead of coming home. Which was fine, but I really wanted to tell you in person." Her words came faster now, her fingers still clutching the denim of his jeans above his knee. "After that, I figured I'd settle for any night when we were together. Except the next time you were due for a home game, your goalie was getting traded and you went on the road to talk the new guy into signing with your team. Remember?"

He recalled. Hurt for her and what she'd gone through alone wound with the hurt he felt now. Yes, he'd been trying to arrange help for his ailing mom at the same time, but he hadn't shared that with her either. Could he blame her for shouldering the pregnancy news alone?

"I wish you'd called me. I know telling me over the phone wouldn't have been ideal, but at least I would have known." His throat burned with what might have been, even if only for a short while. He could have known about his child, had the opportunity to place his hand on Lark's stomach. Over their baby. "I could have alerted the team that I needed to be there for you. They would have made sure your call got through that night of the charity event if I'd told them you were newly pregnant."

"I know," she said softly, her hand sliding off his knee. She swiveled away from him on the counter stool and took a sip of the tea he'd made her. "One of my many regrets the night I miscarried was that I didn't let you know about the baby. Afterward, it seemed cruel to tell you when we couldn't change the outcome."

"So you packed up and left." He'd never forget the cold, echoing foyer of the home they'd shared with her boxes stacked and waiting for the moving truck.

But he'd allowed the hurt he'd felt to prevent him from going after her. From demanding answers about why she was leaving. He'd assumed it was because he hadn't been home enough.

After a childhood with a father who'd never found anything redeeming in him, Gibson had grown the thick skin that had allowed him to thrive in his sport. But it had prevented him from forming deep attachments. Something he'd sought professionally counseling for, once upon a time. Except that when he'd walked into the therapist's office, he'd seen Lark and wanted to date her more than he wanted counseling.

No doubt he'd been just as glad to set aside the idea of therapy in favor of romance with the sexiest woman he'd ever seen. But he'd done them both a disservice that day.

"I'm sorry I didn't tell you before," Lark said finally, slipping off the stool to loop the strap of her cross-body bag over one shoulder. "I should have explained myself to you long before now. Being in Catamount again, and seeing my sisters grow to be stronger people capable of loving relationships, has made me want to be a better person, too."

He recognized the blame wasn't all hers. But did

it matter now when they'd already tried and failed to be together? What if love wasn't enough?

The last thing he wanted was to hurt her again.

For that matter, he wasn't sure he could survive losing her a second time when their divorce had been so painful.

"I'm glad you told me now so we can both have closure." He would be thinking about what might have been for a long time.

He didn't ask her again about attending Jessamyn's wedding together. Part of him wondered if she'd told him about the pregnancy now in order to push him away because she was afraid of getting too close to him again.

For all he knew, maybe that was for the best. Hadn't he promised himself he wouldn't hurt her again?

So when Lark pivoted on her heel and quietly let herself out of his back door, he didn't follow her.

Thirteen

Lark had to dig deep into her emotional resources to fulfill her co–maid of honor role with the grace it deserved. Dressed in the stunning navy blue gown that, until today, only Gibson had seen her wearing, she rushed up the stairs at Crooked Elm with a glass of water and some crackers for the pregnant bride who was getting dressed for the big day.

"Here you go, Jess." She called out to her sister as she entered the largest bedroom in the house that now legally belonged to them. Before today, none of the Barclay sisters had used this particular space since it had been inhabited by their grandmother. Instead, Fleur, Lark and Jessamyn had gravitated to the smaller rooms they'd occupied as children when they'd visited the Colorado ranch. But in their planning sessions for the wedding, Fleur had declared their grandmother's former chamber as the best place for a bridal suite. Jessamyn and Lark had agreed it would be a wonderful way to make new memories in the space, and to feel like Gran was with them.

"I've got your morning sickness cure."

She crossed the dark plank floor, the grapefruit-colored walls providing a vibrant backdrop for the bride dressed in her ivory chiffon, off-the-shoulder gown.

Fleur scurried around the hem of the dress, fluffing the fabric so that Lark had intermittent peeks at Jessamyn's hand-stitched ivory lace shoes where she stood in front of the antique cheval mirror. Fleur had draped the mirror with one of Gran's white lace mantillas so that Jessamyn's reflection was surrounded by the fabric.

Seeing her framed that way made a lump form in Lark's throat. She told herself to focus on her sisters and the beauty of the moment, not the memories of her own love story gone so far awry. But how could she not remember her own wedding today?

These weeks in Catamount with Gibson had made her remember all the ways they'd been good together. He'd supported her through the trial. Applauded her courage in standing up to the media. Given her a safe haven from them when she'd wanted a retreat.

And then, there'd been the hours in his bed when everything else had fallen away and their love—because yes, that's still what she'd shared with him—had been the only thing in the world.

"I'm feeling better now that I started to move around again," Jessamyn declared, waving away the cracker offering, her French manicure showing off her engagement ring on her right hand, where it would remain until Ryder slid the wedding band on her left. Then, she would transfer the pear-shaped diamond to her left finger as well, fitting the V-shaped platinum pieces together. "The scent of the hair spray just made me a little woozy."

"I'm glad your stomach settled," Lark said briskly, setting the silver tray on the bedside table near a framed photo of the Barclay sisters when they were girls. "Because it's almost time to head downstairs."

Her gaze lingered on the old picture of herself at thirteen, standing next to one of the four-rail fences to support six-year-old Fleur as she leaned to stroke the nose of a buckskin-colored mustang. Jessamyn would have been nine at the time, and she had one foot on the fence to stroke the horse's neck on the other side of the animal. All three of them looked thoroughly happy, cheeks pink from the summer sun and fresh air, hair in careless ponytails and feet in matching turquoise-colored cowboy boots, a gift from Gran that year. She'd loved those boots.

She made a mental note to buy new pairs for herself and her sisters, too. She might not be staying in Catamount, but she could take that happy memory home with her, along with the knowledge that her sisters would enjoy them. Her visit to Colorado had returned her to her family, and that was a very good thing, no matter how much she hurt today for the love that had slipped away from her.

Again.

"It's that time already?" Fleur stood, her face flushed from all the gown straightening. Her navy blue dress was styled differently than Lark's, the strapless sweetheart neckline and slight flare to her skirt giving her dress a more overtly feminine appeal that suited the former rodeo queen. She peered out the window overlooking the yard where wedding guests had been arriving for the last twenty minutes. "Oh be still, my heart. The men are a sight to behold."

Lark's heart smarted at the thought of the man who was missing from the small ceremony. The ex-husband who hadn't wanted his date with her after learning how she'd robbed him of those weeks where he could have—albeit briefly—celebrated the news of being a father.

She hadn't told her sisters about the split with Gibson since she'd never mentioned that sparks had been flying between them throughout her stay in Catamount. It was easier that way.

Although, even as she thought it, she wondered if she was once again robbing herself of the chance to share her hurts and maybe find better healing. She'd done the same thing with Gibson. But she was saved from having to overthink that realization when a new voice spoke from the threshold of the bedroom.

"Is there room for one more in here?"

Jennifer Barclay stepped tentatively inside, wearing an elegantly draped blue mother-of-the-bride dress, the silk hand-painted with swirls of cream and tan. Far from matronly, the dress skimmed her curves to show off an enviable form. Her dark hair was in a sleek twist, while pearl and gold earrings winked in the sunlight as she gazed at Jessamyn.

The daughter she'd only just begun to reconnect with after the family rift.

"Of course there's room," Jessamyn replied as she waved her inside. "Mom, you look beautiful."

"No, honey. You're the one who is absolutely radiant." Striding deeper into the bridal suite, their mother stopped in front of the bride to admire the ivory chiffon wedding gown. "I can't tell you how happy I am to be a part of your day."

Lark knew the two of them had made steps toward healing their relationship, and she hoped today would cement the progress since Jessamyn had asked her mother to walk her down the aisle. Their father had opted not to attend the wedding even though Jessamyn hadn't revoked his invitation.

Mateo Barclay hadn't spoken to them since he'd left town after losing the ranch.

Now, Jessamyn stepped forward to take her mom's hands in hers. "I'm really happy, too. Especially now that I'm going to be a mother." She gave a self-deprecating smile. "I'll have a new take on the mother-daughter relationship now."

Mom squeezed her hands before spinning to face all three of them. "You'll be a wonderful mother. Better than I've been."

All three of them opened their mouths to argue,

but their mom shook her head, cutting them off. "No, listen to me. I had a duty to my family, and I failed you all when my life went off the rails once your father left us."

Lark refused to be silent. "Mom, you were ill. No one can fault you for depression. We had a duty to you, too."

She'd tried to be there for her mother. But Jennifer Barclay's road to wellness had been a long one, worsened by setbacks with her personal life. Lark realized now it might have helped her mother more if she'd reached out to Jessamyn herself, to be a good older sister and substitute maternal figure through Jennifer's illness. Instead, Lark had been too wrapped up in anger with her sibling.

"I know that, sweetheart. I've accepted that I couldn't change my illness. But it doesn't take away the fact that I checked out of my job as a mother during those years." As she spoke, a warm breeze stirred the curtains behind her, even lifting the lace mantilla to flutter softly.

All their eyes went to the movement.

Lark wasn't the superstitious sort, but even she saw it as a sign. Gran was there. Approving of the moment. Being a part of this day.

Fleur cleared her throat, her gray gaze bright with emotion. "I think Gran is saying that it's okay. We forgive each other, and we all want to do better. To *be* better for one another."

And they were, Lark knew. She'd tried harder this week, reserving judgment, not assuming a negative motive on anyone else's part, and it had paid off. She was in this wedding, a part of Jessamyn's life once more.

What if she'd tried that hard in other areas of her life? Like with Gibson?

Her mother stepped forward, reaching a hand out to Fleur and Jessamyn, who in turn both reached out to Lark. So they stood in an unbroken circle of four. From the backyard, strains of country love songs drifted through the window from a guitar and fiddle player who'd been hired for the day.

It was almost time for the vows.

Drawing a deep breath, her mom spoke softly. "Each of you has filled me with pride in your own way. You might seem different from one another on the surface, but in your hearts, you're all strong, independent women, brave enough to live the lives you imagined for yourselves. That takes courage."

Lark felt a twinge at the words that were meant as a compliment but felt hollow for her personally. She could see how her sisters had done that. Fleur had taken a chance by coming to Catamount with nothing but her dreams of owning a restaurant, determined to sell the property for a profit so she had the resources to start her business. But she'd adapted her dream to encompass the town and the man she'd grown to love.

Jessamyn, too, had followed her heart to Catamount, and now she was planning to use her real estate development skills to initiate agritourism in the area, finding ways to showcase Ryder's off-grid living initiatives in ways that would inspire others. She had plans for self-sustaining yurts in a range of wilderness locations so tourists could experience the beauty of the region as well as a commitment to the land.

All while preparing to have a baby.

But what had Lark done besides show up for the wedding and make nice with her siblings? She was planning to catch a flight in the morning to return to Los Angeles. Was that really living the life of her dreams? Or had she been playing it safe with Gibson, pushing him away before he could hurt her?

Yes, her parents' disastrous marriage had made her gun-shy. But she'd told herself she'd grown beyond that when she took a chance on romance and married Gibson. When the going got hard, however, had she fought for her dreams? Or their shared dreams?

Not by a long shot. She'd cut and run, scared he wouldn't be there to support her when she needed him. Afraid to give him a second chance after he hadn't rushed to her side on that night she'd needed him.

But she wasn't the same woman that she used to be. Two years apart had only reinforced that Gibson was the only one for her. And she'd had time to appreciate the way her sisters has fostered the love in their lives, even when there were obstacles.

She needed more courage. Before today, she hadn't known where to find it. Yet right now, feeling the love of her family around her in a way she hadn't experienced in over a decade, Lark felt a welling up of new fortitude.

And yes, love.

She had more to give, and she wasn't going to leave Catamount without trying harder to live her dreams with Gibson at her side.

After the circle of four disbanded, Lark, her mom and sisters picked up their bouquets and descended the stairs.

Lark was the last one to step outside into the sunshine while the guitarist picked out the strains of a wedding march. Ahead of her, forty white folding chairs adorned with tulle and flowers sat in rows facing an arbor with four rough log posts where an officiant waited to perform the ceremony. The posts were draped in pink roses, white hydrangeas and grape hyacinths, the stems wrapped in clouds of white tulle. More white tulle fluttered around the top of the posts to provide a thin canopy from the sun.

The effect was country elegance, a perfect blend of Jessamyn's refined preferences and her love of Western life. Ryder waited for her under the canopy in a dark gray suit, an ivory rose boutonniere complementing the bride.

With every fiber of her being, she wished that Gibson was in the crowd waiting for her. Looking toward her with even a fraction of the feeling that she could see in the groom's eyes as he awaited his bride.

Then, as Lark blinked into the brightness of the day, her eyes adjusting to the noontime sun, she spotted a tall, broad-shouldered figure sliding into one of the white folding chairs.

A heart-achingly familiar figure.

Was it just a wishful imagining of a heart tied in knots by the romance of the day?

Hurrying to stand beside Fleur for their procession up the white carpet to the arbor, Lark couldn't take her eyes off those shoulders. An athlete's unmistakable, well-muscled form. Just like in the courtroom day after day, he'd shown up today when she'd needed him.

Was he quietly making up for the way he hadn't always been around while they were married? For weeks, he'd been showing her a different side of himself and she'd been too caught up in her own fears to recognize that he'd changed. She'd accused him of always putting his team first, but for the last year— even when he'd still been on the active roster for his club—hadn't he been overseeing his mother's transition to living with him? She'd seen firsthand how much thought he put into making a comfortable home for her, providing her with both love and security. Even providing himself with an outlet in the mountain retreat for days when caregiving grew more difficult.

Not to mention, all his plans for a future outside of hockey with a bison ranch. His future wouldn't be tied to a sport, and that had to be a tough transition for him.

He was changing. But had she changed enough to make a relationship between them really work?

When Gibson rose to his feet to watch the processional, she was staring at him when their eyes locked.

Held.

And she hoped some of the day's wedding magic

would rub off on her so that, after the ceremony, she could find the words to convince him to give their love one more chance.

She still took his breath away.

Gibson watched the subtle sway of Lark's hips as she made her way up the aisle, her navy blue silk dress molding to her curves whenever the breeze blew. He wouldn't approach her today since she'd made it clear that he wasn't her date. But Drake had invited him, and he wouldn't ignore the duty to a friend, so he sat in the back. Alone.

His eyes returning to Lark again and again. She'd worn her dark hair half-up and half-down, forget-me-nots woven through a braid coiled at the back of her head while the rest of the tresses fell over her shoulders, hiding the mostly backless dress.

He'd always liked that about her. The subtlety of her beauty that was never showy, as if she reserved it for those who took the time to pay attention.

And man, did he ever pay attention to this woman as she settled into her place beside her sister for the ceremony. Even as the officiant spoke, Gibson kept his focus on Lark. He'd shortchanged her during their marriage, taking her strength and independence for granted. But just because she could deal with whatever life threw at her didn't mean she should have to. She'd deserved a partner who put her first.

Something he would do now that he'd learned to draw his own boundaries. To step away from the old pattern of being the best, being the guy his team could count on. The people he loved were important than the game.

His mom.

And yes, Lark.

His thoughts were interrupted by the sound of Ryder's voice as he faced his bride.

"I give this ring as a sign of my love." The words rang out over the yard, the guy's eyes fixed, unwavering, on Jessamyn Barclay as he lowered the band into place on her left finger.

While he spoke his vows, Gibson's gaze sought Lark's. Was she remembering their wedding day, too?

He thought of the vows he'd spoken four years ago, and how deeply he'd meant them. Yet he hadn't delivered on them when push came to shove. He hadn't been there for Lark when she'd needed him. Hadn't let himself need her either, always so damned confident he could take care of his own problems thanks to his father's earliest admonitions that a hockey player needed to be invincible.

Which of course, he wasn't.

When it was the bride's turn to speak, Lark's green eyes shifted from his to land on her sibling.

"...to have and to hold, from this day forward, for better or for worse..." Jessamyn's voice was steady as she spoke the words that would unite them as a couple in front of their friends and family.

He hadn't done that with Lark, opting instead for a courthouse ceremony. They'd been deliriously happy at the time, but how could they have known what life would have in store for them? How could they have guessed how much they would need the support of a network like this one—people who'd born witness to the vows?

With the ache in his chest deepening with every word spoken, Gibson couldn't wait for the end of the ceremony. His time he had to win back the woman he loved was running out, with her flight leaving in the morning.

So as soon as the officiant announced the couple as husband and wife, and the musical duo began a triumphant wedding recessional song, Gibson calculated the fastest way to win an audience with Lark.

There was no receiving line with such a small wedding. The reception would begin soon, with an informal meal under a nearby canopy. But for now, the wedding guests simply congregated around the newlyweds, offering congratulations and teasing marital advice. With Fleur as Lark's co–maid of honor, those duties would be covered for a few minutes if he could sneak a little time to speak to Lark privately.

Except, in the shifting crowd around the bride and groom, he'd somehow lost sight of her.

"Looking for someone?" a woman's voice asked to his left.

Glancing down, he saw Jennifer Barclay, Lark's mother.

"So good to see you, er, Mrs. Barclay." He'd briefly called this woman "Mom" when he and Lark had been married. While Lark had been comfortable calling his mother by her first name, Gibson had opted to move right to the more familial name for her mother. "And yes, I was looking for Lark."

"I had the feeling you were." She beamed, her expression happy and her cheeks glowing. No doubt she was pleased to have mended the rift with Jessamyn. "She asked me to let you know that she's waiting for you by the creek. She seemed to think you'd know where she meant."

Lark had asked to see him?

"I do." He told himself it might not mean anything. Maybe she only wished to say goodbye privately. But he couldn't help hoping that this could be a sign she wanted something more. "Before I talk to her though, do you have any advice for winning her back? That is, if I promise to be a much better partner for her in the future?"

He had no way of knowing what her mother thought of him and the role he'd played in their breakup. But he wasn't going to shy away anymore from asking for help when he needed it. And there was nothing more important to him now than telling Lark how much he wanted to try again.

Nearby, a server recruited from the Cowboy Kitchen strolled past with a wooden tray of champagne glasses. Lark's mom took one, but Gibson wasn't ready to celebrate yet.

"Gibson, I always thought you were a good balance for Lark." She lay a hand on his arm as if she could impress her thoughts on him. "Before she met you, she worked nonstop, as if she needed permission to have fun. But when you were together, I saw her take time away for vacations with you and for road trips to your games."

He'd forgotten about that. Once he'd moved to the Los Angeles team and taken on its problems as his own, his marriage had suffered.

"I appreciate you saying that." His gaze lifted toward the path to the feeder creek for the White River, where Lark waited for him even now. "I hope I can convince her to give me another chance."

"I won't claim to be an expert on love, but I do know my daughter." Mrs. Barclay smiled, her face shifting in a way that made the resemblance to her oldest daughter clear. "And I can't help but think you should speak from the heart when you talk to her. Lark has enough practicality in her life. She deserves to be wooed with romance and flowers. A man who sees past her tough exterior to the sweet and vulnerable woman beneath."

It was sound advice, and it settled around him with a new rightness. He'd gotten to know Lark better this week too, and he'd been reminded of her deeply tender side. She'd talked to his mom for almost an hour about her doll collection, patiently listening to the stories from Stephanie Vaughn's childhood to learn how she'd acquired each one. And she'd done it while she'd had every right to be angry with him, right after she'd learned that he hadn't confided in her about the severity of his mom's disease progression.

"You're right." Leaning down, he kissed his former mother-in-law on the cheek—hopefully soon to be his current and forever mother-in-law. "I'm going to do just that."

Spinning away, he started toward the tree line to find Lark.

Trailing a long blade of feathery reed grass across the surface of the creek, Lark had started to get nervous Gibson wasn't coming when she finally heard the sound of pine needles crunching underfoot.

Branches slapping against a body moving through them.

She tensed, equal parts hope and anxiety twisting her insides. Turning, she spotted Gibson in his dark suit and white shirt just a few yards from her. Through the trees behind him, she could still see the wedding party on the lawn. The white canopy set up for the meal with a few picnic tables on loan. The huge floral arbor where Jessamyn had said her vows.

The music carried easily, upbeat country tunes but no vocals. Later, her sister and Ryder would test their country waltzing skills, but for now, the guests milled around with cocktails and passed hors d'oeuvres.

"You're going to ruin your shoes," Gibson warned her, his dark gaze going to her feet where she stood in the tall grass.

"Nope." Lifting the hem of her dress, she showed him a pair of her old cowboy boots. "I grabbed a pair of these from the porch before I walked here."

"Very practical," he admitted, his attention shifting to her hand where she still held the long reed grass. "But you're still going to get your gown wet if you're not careful."

Releasing the slender reed, she wiped her hands together and shrugged. "Maybe. But at least I got through the ceremony looking like I belonged in this dress. I don't think Jessamyn will be surprised if I return with a few wrinkles."

"You can take the girl out of the country, but you can't take the country out of the girl?"

She smiled. "Something like that." Her smile faded again as she realized... "Although technically, I'm supposed to leave this part of the country tomorrow."

"I want to speak to you about that." He took a step closer to her, his big body parting the reed grasses until he stood toe-to-toe with her.

Her breath caught at his nearness, the cedar and sandalwood scent of his aftershave teasing her nostrils. Her heartbeat jumped erratically.

"Actually, it was me who wanted to talk to you regarding that. My mother must have told you?" Nervous, she brushed one palm along the top of the fluffy reed grass, the tiny filaments tickling her skin.

He frowned. "She told me where to find you but didn't say what you wanted."

Hadn't she told her mother that she hoped to have another chance with Gibson? But then, Jennifer Barclay had displayed a huge amount of confidence in Lark and her sisters this weekend. It had been nice when Mom talked about being proud of them, touching a part of her soul she hadn't realized had been hungry to hear words like that.

Perhaps her mother had been sure Lark could handle the situation on her own.

And live the life she'd imagined for herself.

"For starters, I wanted to say that I've learned a lot about myself this month. About where I went wrong in our marriage." She hesitated a moment, still uneasy about sharing the full extent of her insights. But was that being brave? Living courageously?

"Lark, I made the mistakes," he said somberly. "Far more than you ever—"

"Please, let me just say this." If she wanted a better relationship, she needed to take bigger risks. She could even picture herself telling her patients as much. Why hadn't she taken the advice seriously for herself? "After telling you about the miscarriage, I wondered if part of the reason I'd kept it to myself for so long was just another way to keep you at arm's length. To not risk being..." She had to pause to clear her throat, and when she spoke, the words were raspy. "Vulnerable with you again."

Gibson's warm palms moved to her shoulders bared by the thin spaghetti straps of her gown. His fingers flexed into her skin, and she had to close her eyes against how good it felt to have him touch her.

"And that's understandable. I wish I had been a better man for you while we were married, but I wasn't present enough for us to build the kind of relationship I think we both wanted." His thumbs sketched small circles on her arms where he touched her, soothing and inciting at the same time.

"It's not understandable, Gibson. It was wrong

of me." She'd been so upset with herself—and him, too—that she hadn't been able to face the mistake. Not then, and not for a long time afterward.

It had been easier to run than to face all the frustrations she'd suppressed in her marriage. To articulate her hurt and work toward solutions. She'd told herself she'd handled the breakup well—better than her parents had survived the dissolution of their relationship. But she'd only been holding it together on the surface. Deep inside, she'd fallen apart, too.

In spite of all her precautions not to let love wreck her.

"You're too hard on yourself." He pulled her into his arms now, surrounding her with his strength and warmth. His scent.

She breathed him in, grateful for the chance to be close. Grateful that he'd listened to her and didn't hate her for keeping the news of his child from him.

After a long moment, she realized he was stroking her hair over the middle of her back, his cheek pressed to her temple. And nothing in her life had ever felt as right as being in his arms.

Angling back from him, she laid her palms on his chest, feeling the expensive silk of his suit. The warm heart beating beneath. Taking a slow breath, she reminded herself that she was here to take risks. To live the life of her dreams.

"I don't want to leave Catamount."

Her words were met with silence as he stared at her. His eyebrows lifting. Jaw working slowly as if he was warming up to speak.

Her stomach twisted. Her chest ached where she craved this man's love.

At last, he lifted a hand to her face and tilted it upward another degree.

"I don't want you to leave Catamount either. Not tomorrow. Not ever. Unless you take me with you wherever you go." His thumb grazed her cheekbone, rubbing lightly.

Her pulse leapt. And she suspected her eyebrows were the ones arching high now. Because she had not expected this for even one second.

"What?" She shook her head to clear her ears, her heart hammering too loudly for her to hear him over the whoosh of it echoing in her head. "What are you saying?"

She tried to listen hard. In her degree program, she'd learned about generous listening, where you opened your mind to people without anticipating what they would say or how you would respond. It was a tool she used often in her practice, and she leaned into it now to hear what Gibson was saying, because it was wildly different from how she'd expected this conversation to go.

"I love you, Lark. I don't think I ever stopped loving you." He spoke with a gravity she'd never heard from him before, a sincerity that matched up with the dark intensity of his eyes.

Hope sparked brighter. Still, she had to be sure. "But when I left your house the other night, I thought—"

"I didn't handle the news well, but mostly because

I was so disappointed with myself for not being the man you needed me to be while we were married. That you couldn't even have me in the same room as you to share your pregnancy news—news that would have been so welcomed—it hit home what a rotten husband I'd been."

On the lawn behind the trees, a roar of laughter went up over the romantic melody of the guitar and fiddle. A champagne cork popped, and then another and another.

"That's not true." She'd been frustrated with his travel and with the media, but despite their problems, she'd never stopped loving him. "When we were together, I was happy. And I thought I was being a good wife not to complain about the long separations, but I know now we owed it to ourselves to find solutions instead of just wading through those hard times."

"I owed you far better than I gave you," he said resolutely. "But you're not the only one who has learned things this month. I know I can do better now."

Excitement tickled along her nerve endings as it occurred to her this was really happening. Gibson Vaughn loved her. He wanted to be with her again.

She couldn't suppress a smile. It bloomed over her face like the new happiness filling her insides.

"I never stopped loving you either. And I already know that you've changed. I saw you in court for me every day even when I pushed you away. And you came to the wedding today when I desperately wanted to see you." She looped her arms around his neck, pressing herself even closer to him.

"You did?" He stroked his fingers through her hair.

A dislodged forget me not drifted to her bare shoulder, and all she could think about was getting through the reception to be alone with him later.

"I did. At first I thought I wished you into being there, but it was really you, turned out in your custom suit, looking all kinds of edible."

His eyes darkened and he bent to brush a kiss over her lips.

"You're the edible one," he breathed the words over her damp mouth. "And I'll prove it to you later."

Desire pooled in her belly even though it was the wrong time for that. They had so much to navigate if they were going to be in one another's lives again, but first they needed to celebrate her sister's big day.

Still, all of that would be a joy because on the other side of it would be Gibson. Not just for a night or a week.

Forever.

A yellow leaf drifted down from a nearby tree, an early sign of fall that came to rest on Gibson's shoulder before she brushed it away.

Summer was ending, and a new chapter of her life would begin. Here in Catamount. In a house next door to both of her sisters. She could work remotely for a while. Start a new practice here.

Become the wife of a bison rancher, which made her smile again.

But all of that would wait until tomorrow.

"We should rejoin the party," she murmured. "Everyone will wonder what happened to us."

"I bet they could guess," he argued, smoothing his hands down to her waist. Over her hips. Lower. "And I don't think anyone will worry."

Her smile returned. She couldn't seem to keep it off her face, not that she wanted to try.

"We're really doing this? Getting back together?" She ran a hand along his freshly shaven jaw. Her heart full.

"If you mean are we really going to be together forever the way we once promised each other we would be?" He lifted her higher against him, so they were eye to eye. "The answer is yes."

"Thank goodness." She tipped her forehead to his, breathing in the man and the moment. "And to be perfectly clear, this time I'm never letting go."

It was his turn to smile as he turned toward the tree line so they could return to the wedding party.

"That's what I was hoping you'd say. Now, it's the perfect day to drink a toast to the happy couple and celebrate happy-ever-afters." Gibson lifted their joined hands to his lips so he could lay a very deliberate kiss on the ring finger of her left hand.

Where a ring used to be.

She knew him so well. She felt the promise in that kiss. Knew that a ring would rest there again one day.

For now, she simply planned to celebrate this love they shared, the love they couldn't walk away from.

Every. Single. Day.

* * * * *

WE HOPE YOU ENJOYED
THIS BOOK FROM

✦HARLEQUIN
DESIRE

*Luxury, scandal, desire—welcome to
the lives of the American elite.*

Be transported to the worlds of oil barons, family dynasties,
moguls and celebrities. Get ready for juicy plot twists,
delicious sensuality and intriguing scandal.

6 NEW BOOKS AVAILABLE EVERY MONTH!

#2893 VACATION CRUSH
Texas Cattleman's Club: Ranchers and Rivals
by Yahrah St. John
What do you do after confessing a crush on an accidental livestream?
Take a vacation to escape the gossip! But when Natalie Hastings gets to
the resort, her crush—handsome rancher Jonathan Lattimore—is there
too. Will one little vacation fling be enough?

#2894 THE MARRIAGE MANDATE
Dynasties: Tech Tycoons • by Shannon McKenna
Pressured into marrying, heiress Maddie Moss chooses the last man in
the world her family will accept—her brother's ex–business partner,
Jack Daly. Accused of destroying the company, Jack can use the
opportunity to finally prove his innocence—but only if he can resist Maddie...

#2895 A RANCHER'S REWARD
Heirs of Hardwell Ranch • by J. Margot Critch
To earn a large inheritance, playboy rancher Garrett Hardwell needs a
fake fiancée—fast! Wedding planner Willa Statler is the best choice. The
problem? She's his best friend's younger sister! With so much at stake, will
their very real connection ruin everything?

#2896 SECOND CHANCE VOWS
Angel's Share • by Jules Bennett
Despite their undeniable chemistry, Camden Preston and Delilah Hawthorn
are separating. With divorce looming, Delilah is shocked when her blind
date at a masquerade gala turns out to be her husband! The attraction's
still there, but can they overcome what tore them apart?

#2897 BLACK SHEEP BARGAIN
Billionaires of Boston • by Naima Simone
Abandoned at birth, CEO Nico Morgan will upend the one thing his father
loved most—his company. Integral to the plan is a charming partner, and
that's his ex, Athena Evans. But old feelings and hot passion could derail
everything...

#2898 SECRET LIVED AFTER HOURS
The Kane Heirs • by Cynthia St. Aubin
Finding his father's assistant at an underground fight club, playboy
Mason Kane realizes he isn't the only one leading a double life. So he
offers Charlotte Westbrook a whirlwind Riviera fling to help her loosen up,
but it could cost her job and her heart...

HDCNM0722

"This won't work. You know it won't." Felicity continued. "If the baby is your priority, then you and I can't…"

Can't what?" Wynn smiled mockingly.

"You're taunting me, but I don't know why."

"You don't want to *enjoy* each other while you're here?"

"We had our chance. We didn't make it work. And I'm not one for fooling around just for a few orgasms."

"The old Fliss never said things like that."

"The old *Felicity* was an eighteen-year-old kid."

"You always seemed mature for your age. You had a vision for your future and you made it happen. I'm proud of you."

She gaped at him. "Thank you."

"I'm sorry," he said gruffly. "I shouldn't have kissed you. Let's pretend it never happened. A fresh start, Fliss. Please?"

"Of course. We're both here to honor Shandy and care for her daughter. I don't think we should do anything to mess that up."

"Agreed."

Don't miss what happens next in...
The Comeback Heir
by USA TODAY *bestselling author Janice Maynard.*

Available September 2022 wherever
Harlequin Desire books and ebooks are sold.

Harlequin.com

Love Harlequin romance?

DISCOVER.

Be the first to find out about promotions,
news and exclusive content!

f Facebook.com/HarlequinBooks

Twitter.com/HarlequinBooks

Instagram.com/HarlequinBooks

Pinterest.com/HarlequinBooks

You Tube YouTube.com/HarlequinBooks

ReaderService.com

EXPLORE.

Sign up for the Harlequin e-newsletter and
download a free book from any series at
TryHarlequin.com

CONNECT.

Join our Harlequin community to
share your thoughts and connect
with other romance readers!
Facebook.com/groups/HarlequinConnection

HSOCIAL2021

HARLEQUIN

Heartfelt or thrilling, passionate or uplifting—Harlequin is more than just happily-ever-after.

With twelve different series to choose from and new books available every month, you are sure to find stories that will move you, uplift you, inspire and delight you.

**IF YOU ENJOYED THIS BOOK
WE THINK YOU WILL ALSO LOVE**

◇ HARLEQUIN

PRESENTS

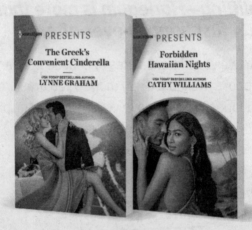

Escape to exotic locations where passion knows no bounds.

Welcome to the glamorous lives of royals and billionaires, where passion knows no bounds. Be swept into a world of luxury, wealth and exotic locations.

8 NEW BOOKS AVAILABLE EVERY MONTH!